Divine
Intervention

KENT GEORGE

ISBN-10: 151741752X
ISBN-13: 978-1517417529

DEDICATION

I would like to dedicate this creation to my future self. Let this book serve as testimony that thoughts are as real as the air we breathe! I would also like to dedicate this creation to any and everybody that can relate to any part of this story. As I was creating this project, I knew that the reader would initially think that this was an autobiography. This is in fact, a fictional novel with a clear message:

"The decisions you make on the daily basis, no matter how big or small, shape your world! Being poor is a mindset, not a financial issue. Rid your mind of all foolishness, because the brain is powerful. Only with a clear mind do things mirror themselves undistorted!"

CONTENTS

ACKNOWLEDGEMENTS

First and foremost; I would like to thank God, who is my Father and Creator for putting me in perfect alignment with all things pure and whole! I would also like to thank my whole team over at King Kent Productions. Last but not least, I would like to thank every experience in my life, good and bad, because it shaped and inspired my art.

I

The world is a stage full of characters of many roles – some bigger than others but definitely a piece to a puzzle that is usually misunderstood because it comes from a higher power. I'm not the most religious person in the world; In fact, I believe that religion is exactly what we make it, but I am a firm believer in John 3:16. I'm definitely a God fearing man. I'm not perfect. Couldn't be if I tried. I like to think of myself as a perfect imperfection! We all are. We as a people need something to believe in, even if it's just believing in yourself. I mean, that's the reason we wake up in the morning. The day you don't have a reason is the day you shouldn't live. Kind of harsh I know, but if you don't have a reason to live then why should you? Most people spend their whole lives searching for that purpose only to find that life's obstacles can knock you so far down that it makes you question why you were even born. I've been there.

The Evils: When the light gets so overshadowed with adversity that the darkness becomes attractive. A place so low that it makes you change your logic and reasoning. See, I understand that circumstance can alter decision making, so I try my best not to judge. Even the bible says there's a time to kill. So "right from wrong" is just another overrated phrase to me.

Do you call a man a killer that killed to protect his family? Or do you call a woman a murderer for having an abortion after she was raped? I guess it's all what you believe is right. But that can easily be influenced by circumstance.

Take culture for example. The single handed, most controversial topic in the world that's always overlooked! Culture comes from location. A city can be 30 minutes from yours but be complete opposites. Kind of funny and sad at the same time. Growing up in Atlanta, Georgia, as it is in most cities and states, the Eastside, Westside, Southside, and Northside are all 15 to 20 minutes away from one another, give or take a few minutes. They are all culturally different from one another from the way they dress all the way down to the music they listen to. We all know people who would take pride in where they're from. Say it loud and proud because in a sense it makes us who we are.

I tend to think of the world as a "concrete jungle." Simply because humans are animals.

Our ways are similar: territorial and to a certain extent, willing to die for respect in what we believe in. I'm especially fascinated by lions, "the kings of the jungle." They're at the top of the food chain but they're not even the biggest animals in the jungle. In relation to humans, a lion raises his pride, or family, to the best of his ability, leaving his son with the understanding that when he dies, his throne will be passed on to him, making him the king of the same jungle. It's something that's just genetically in them that gives them the courage or the heart to even feel that way. Some humans raise their children to be lions, and some are raised to be other animals. A lion has a totally different structure from the next animal living within the same jungle, just as humans do. Just as close. All living within the same jungle, but are so culturally different, from the way or things that they eat, to their outlook on what they are and what they can do. When this is questioned or when they meet one another, death is usually the outcome. Animals! We're all some type of animal. It's all food for thought. That's exactly what we are going through in the concrete jungle. We all have different ways and opinions measured solely by what we believe in which are based on how we were raised and the things we went through. I believe we call those morals. From this, there's an infinite amount of stories to be told. Some are just more interesting than others.

Life is just a big movie, here's mine.

I was born in October of 1983 in Brooklyn, New York. I'm a "Lucky Libra" some say. The Libra sign is a scale which means we go through our whole lives searching for that perfect balance between good and evil; probably not that extreme, but definitely describes my life a bit!

The name King has so much significance behind it. I'm my mother's first born and my father's first son. My mother was only 17 when she birthed me, just a child herself. She was only in the eleventh grade. My mother was the youngest of five girls. She was the baby, so of course she was the spoiled one. My Grandmother on my mother's side passed away while my mother was still pregnant with me. My father was older. He had a passion for the game of basketball with more than enough talent to make it to the NBA. They say all men are created equal, but growing up on the Southside of Jamaica, Queens, that's hard to believe. Taught to survive, my dad was involved in things that pushed basketball to the back. He was a hustler, a certified dope boy. "The black sheep of the family" as he would say. He wasn't your everyday drug dealer though. Naw, see he was a five percenter. His way of life was totally different from the next man. He believed that you survive by any means necessary, literally! Similar to Malcolm Xs' infamous saying, but with his own logic added to it. Nothing to be proud of or glorify, just things had to be done and he was willing to do them without a conscience just a righteous cause.

My father spoiled me. He lived in Queens while my mother attended high school in Brooklyn. I still hear stories to this day of how I used to run out of my apartment building whenever I saw him from the window up the street. Every time I saw my father, he came bearing gifts. I mean EVERY TIME! I got things kids my age probably didn't have any business having at the time. I look at my baby pictures and I'm clothed in labels like Gucci, Izod, Oshkosh, Triple Fat Goose, etc. I was wearing accessories such as rings, fat gold chains and ropes. I even had my ears pierced with little diamond studs.

See, I come from what they call in New York "The Raegan Era", also known as, "The Crack Era". At the time, Ronald Raegan was the President of the United States, and crack was the new drug! My pops was a certified hustler so I reaped the material benefits as the son of a Kingpin! I was the Prince to his throne. My little brother was born a couple years later, followed by another. We all are two years apart. My mother wasn't doing so good and used to leave us at the house a lot while she did whatever it was that she was doing at the time. But as a child growing up in the projects, you tend to grow up real fast so she knew we could take care of ourselves till she got back. One thing about growing up in the projects, well in my building, people always looked out for each other. It could be something as simple as borrowing sugar. No one felt above one another because at the end of the day, we all were living in the same projects with somewhat similar situations. Since everyone came from similar situations, when my mother would leave, she would have Mrs. Sally, our neighbor, look out and keep an eye on us until she got back. In return, my mother would do things like give her food stamps, braid her hair, or sometimes pay her.

Since I was the oldest, and my mother was still a child herself, we had a different type of relationship, a different bond. But she never talked to me like I was a child. She taught and expected me to do things damn near at the same pace that she did them. I caught on fast never knowing that she was just prepping me for the world but later in life found an appreciation that I still can't explain to this day. I love my mother with all my heart but things would soon change and take a turn for the worse!

My aunt, my mother's oldest sister, used to take care of us during the week while my mother worked and attended school. She lived in Queens. She was married with a family of her own. A son and a daughter who were my first cousins. They both were older and my brothers and I spent a lot of time out there with them. They treated us like we were their own kids.

I was a kid and didn't have a single worry in the world. I was always smiling from ear to ear. They nicknamed me kool-aid because of the kool-aid logo in the commercials that was always smiling. Just happy to be alive I guess. That would soon change.

One day, while we were back in Brooklyn, our apartment building caught on fire and the whole building had to evacuate. My mother wasn't home and I was taught to not open the door for anybody except for my father. I didn't even know the building was on fire. I was five years old and I remember it as if it happened last night. Till this day I have nightmares about it, waking up in cold sweats. It's just one of the many scorned images on my brain that to me was the beginning of another life.

It started with an alarming banging at the door that scared me because I

4

immediately knew something was wrong. As a child, we all can sense things – right from wrong, danger and safety. So when I heard the banging, I didn't say anything. Not only because I was scared, but because I didn't know what to do. When my mother used to leave us at the house, my father had a key so he never knocked and Mrs. Sally always called before she came over. I heard the banging again and I knew something was wrong. I looked out the peep hole and it was Mrs.

Sally. She yelled my name at least three times to the top of her lungs but all I could think about was my mother saying "DON'T OPEN THE DOOR FOR ANYBODY BUT YOUR FATHER!" So I didn't.

Mrs. Sally yelled again, "Is anybody in there?! The building is on fire!!!

That's when I replied, "I'm here but I can't open the door. My mother told me not to!"

As I was saying that, I noticed smoke coming through the door. My brothers were asleep but the banging woke them up along with the smoke. I was scared so I tried to open the door and I couldn't for some reason. The door was hot. Every time I touched the doorknob it burned my hands. That's when I started to panic. My youngest brother was only six months old at the time so he was crying louder and louder. My second oldest brother yelled out the window for help as the smoked filled the apartment. I saw Mrs. Sally outside and knew immediately something was wrong. I stepped on a ring running back to the door and my foot started bleeding pretty bad. It didn't hurt but the blood scared my brother and he started crying. Now there was smoke all throughout the apartment and you could feel the heat! I didn't know what to do so I started crying myself. We ran to the window in tears asking for help when all of a sudden there was an even louder banging at the door! We were all scared so we were at the window crying together. I had my youngest brother in my arms and my other brother was right by my side. I didn't know what to do and the banging got louder and louder and louder until the door eventually broke. Not able to see through the smoke, two masked men grabbed us while we were trying to stand on the fire escape out the window. They snatched us right up without saying a word and ran us out of the building. I was so scared that I didn't even realize that they were firemen. There was so much smoke that you couldn't even make out what they were. Come to find out, my mother had locked the door from the inside somehow. I never opened the door while she was gone, so I didn't even know she did that.

While we were downstairs and safe, after crying and nearly dying, somebody told the cops that my mother had left us in the apartments. They took us down to the police station and a social worker came and separated me from my brothers. I cried because I was the oldest and I knew that something was wrong. My mother eventually came down to the station but they wouldn't let her take us home. I didn't see my brothers for hours and that was the longest I could remember going without them. My mother had a conversation with me and it was so vivid that I can still recite every word! She told me that the social workers were going to take us away for a while and she promised me that she would be back to come get us.

I looked at her right in her eyes and I asked her, "Why are you crying?"

She cried to me, "Because I haven't been a good mother and until I get my life together, you're going to have to take care of your brothers for me!"

I mean I was only five years old and I still haven't forgotten the conversation. I asked her, "What about my father? I want my father!!"

I started crying and she held me in her arms and replied, "Your father not ready to have y'all by himself yet, but I promise I'll be back for you! Take care of your brothers and this will all be over soon. I need you to be a big boy for me and remember what I taught you!"

I cried even harder and begged my mother, "Please don't leave me, mommy. I'm scared!"

My mother held my head up, wiped the tears from my eyes and just stared at me in complete silence for about three minutes. Not saying a single word.

And then she told me, "You are my King! I need you to be my strength. My blood is in your heart, so I'll never leave your side! Take care of your brothers till I get back. Promise me!"

And I promised her.

She stared in my eyes for another five minutes and I'll never forget the look she had in her eyes. It was if she knew it was going to be a long time before I saw or heard from her again. Then the social worker came back in and she kissed me on my forehead and left. The police carried her off.

The next day the social worker took my brothers and me into a group foster care home. My brothers and I were split up when we were adopted to different families. I was with an Asian family. They were good to me but I knew this wasn't my home. I cried daily because my life changed drastically. I mean, I wasn't with my mother or my brothers. They were my world and I didn't know when or if I was ever going to see them again.

Eight months had passed and I just got tired of crying! One day I heard a song on the radio that reminded me of my older cousin Shavon. She always sang these crazy songs to my brothers and me that I never took serious until this particular day. The lyrics in the song had how to spell my full name, address, and phone number to my aunt's house. So even though I thought the song was just in fun when I learned it a few years back, it came in handy. I started singing the lyrics in my head over and over to make sure I could remember the words precisely.

Once I remembered the number, I ran to the phone! I dialed the number and I immediately recognized the voice.

"Johnson Residence".

It was Shavon's voice! My heart started pounding fast! I was overwhelmed. This was the first familiar voice I heard in over eight months! We spoke and those conversations soon turned into weekly visits.

My aunt eventually adopted me and my brothers' adoption came shortly after. We were a family again! But I missed my mother. I was old enough to know what exactly took place and even though I was around family, it never felt the same.

II

After about a year of living in Queens, we moved to Atlanta, Georgia. My aunt wanted us to have better opportunities than she did growing up so she felt like a change of scenery was key. Little did she know that growing up on the Eastside of Atlanta, there was little to no difference from where we just moved. New York is fast paced and a fast lifestyle. In an environment like that, you are usually forced to grow up fast. Your innocent childhood meets the harsh reality of being an adult. Atlanta was no different. Not as big, but rapidly growing!

When I started school in Atlanta, it was easy to make friends. I stood out of course because I dressed differently. I remember clear as day having to stand up in front of the class and introduce myself.

"My name is King Brady, but everybody calls me King. I'm from Brooklyn, New York and I am 10 years old. My birthday is this week and my aunt said that I should bring cupcakes to make new friends, but I told her I'll wait to see if you all were friendly!"

The whole class laughed including the teacher, Mrs Curtious.

"That's some accent you have, Mr. Brady. Tell us a little more about yourself. Do you have any brothers or sisters?"

"Well, I have two younger brothers and two older cousins and we all go to the same school. I love having brothers because I'm never bored, but we always fight over clothes and food! I guess that's normal according to the other families I see on T.V. I'm a little nervous right now, Mrs. Curtious. So I'm trying to imagine everybody naked!"

The whole class laughed so hard that I automatically became the talk of the class. I never was the shy type and definitely a bit charismatic. My aunt always told me I had an "old soul." I never really understood exactly what that meant but that didn't stick out to me as much as her saying I'm so nonchalant.

School was easy to me. It actually got a bit boring. I didn't feel challenged. It wasn't that I was so much smarter than the other students, I could just grasp and comprehend things a little quicker. In a way, school was an escape for me. I was old enough to remember the tragic experience that took me away from my mother. I even had nightmares about it. I could remember clear how a year or two earlier I was literally in a foster home. Kids catch on to things fast. It taught me to be observant. I could hear loud and clear conversations of my aunt and mother arguing on the phone because my mother had turned to drugs. I guess life got a bit much for her. It didn't help to hear that my father was in prison either. I was a mature kid with curious questions, so when I asked, I got direct answers without any sugar coating! Sometimes she even took it out on us. Not abusive physically, but verbally said things that probably shouldn't have been said to a kid. So school was a relief to me. It was cool interacting with the other kids, playing sports, and just getting out of the house.

Time went on, and for two years straight I got all A's. That's usually a good thing but for some strange reason my conduct deferred. My teacher called my aunt at home and scheduled a parent teacher meeting. I didn't know what the meeting was about and the fact that Mr. Smith said that I didn't have to be there had me worried! It couldn't be anything too bad, I thought because I had an A in his class. I saw my aunt in the hall and she just told me to wait for her in the car. About 30 minutes went by and my aunt came back to the car.

I cut the radio down and in my most sarcastic voice I asked her, "What's the verdict?" My aunt looked at me and just smiled. "Mr. Smith thinks that you're a smart young man.

Full of potential. He also feels you're too smart for your own good. That's why you get bored with school and cry for attention in other ways, like being the class clown. And he says that's why your conduct is getting worse. He wants you to join this 8 week computer/basketball summer camp that he's a part of. He also wants to mentor you."

In my head I heard everything she said differently. "Cry for attention!? 8 weeks!?? Summer camp!?"

But knowing my aunt, I didn't have a choice anyway so I just accepted the task.

Summer camp came around and Mr. Smith turned out to be a pretty cool guy. He had a son that was my age and a daughter who was two years older than me. They went to private school. Summer camp had students from all around the state ages 12 to14. I was only 11 but since my birthday was in October and Mr. Smith was one of the chairmen, I was able to attend. We lived in co-ed bunks. Of course we all thought that was cool. But there were adult chaperons on every other isle. We were in groups of 10 and my group came up with the nickname "lucky libra" for me. It kind of stuck with me and I liked it because there was a cute 14 year old girl that gave it to me.

The camp was pretty much like regular school split into two parts. The morning part we went to school and they taught us computer programming and coding. The second part of the day, they taught us the fundamentals of basketball. Even exchange I guess, giving the fact they took our WHOLE summer with this nerd camp.

The first two weeks of the nerd camp was terrible! I was home sick and hated it! I hated the fact that I couldn't be home with my brothers, I hated the food, I hated the whole structure of the camp. We even went to school on Saturdays.

I called home daily begging to come home. I tried to find any reason to convince my aunt to come get me from that hell hole.

After a week of pleading with my aunt she finally decided to come check on me. She paid me a surprise weekend visit. She spent the whole day with me. She went to all my classes and even watched us practice basketball drills.

When the day was over, I thought she was going to take me home with her but I was so wrong! My aunt told me that me being there was the Lord's work!

"We couldn't afford to get you here but Mr. Smith believed in you and that's why you're here! You want to come home because this is a change of pace for you. So you're intimidated. Embrace change and make it fun for YOU! I know you understand the work but you feel like it's useless. Make it a challenge! Mr. Smith thinks your autodidact. That means that you learn better on your own. Teachers have different styles and methods of teaching so the way you learn is by studying on your own in your free time! Learn how to decipher the bullshit from what is really important. Picking up the book is your reassurance!"

My aunt had a way with words. She knew exactly what to say to weigh heavily on me. So I decided right then and there to tighten up and make this nerd camp work for me.

As my aunt was leaving, she rolled the window down and said, "I love you! And you looking real good on that basketball court."

I felt good going to camp the following week, until I found out I was the joke of the camp! The other students there saw my aunt's car and had a bunch of jokes. See, the majority of them went to private schools so their parents had money. I thought about it and immediately respected my aunt and uncle that much more because I never even knew we were poor.

And there it was. That was my motivation right there. I instantly knew what I had to do. I wanted to be best person in the camp! After a month of nerd camp, all the foreign numbers started making sense. The numbers started becoming clearer and clearer until it was English to me. Our final project was due in two weeks and we also had a basketball tournament. I decided to come up with a video game for my final project. I spent all my free time calculating the software and playing basketball. I wanted to be the best.

After turning in our final projects, I got an A on my project but only came in 5th place overall out of the whole camp. We also lost in the basketball tournament and came in 5th place. I felt like shit! People tried to cheer me up but there was no making me happy. I was a sore loser!

Before the next school year started, I got a letter in the mail that was promoting me to skip 7th grade and go straight to 8th grade based on my performance in the nerd camp. I was nervous and excited about the idea of skipping ahead to the 8th grade. Excited because it meant that I could try out for the high school basketball team and nervous because I was going to be entering high school two years early! I had grown fond of the game of basketball at the camp because it became a release for me. It was how I vented.

My first week of high school was rough! I could never make it on time to any of my classes. This school was literally five times the size of the elementary school from where I came. I caused a scene three times back to back to back because I had to go to the guidance counselor's office after each class to be escorted to the next class. I also looked different. I was only supposed to be going to the 7th grade, so there were certain things I wasn't going through at all. Like puberty! Oh. And oh my God!! The girls were beautiful. They all looked grown. I remember walking through the lunch room like I was in paradise. I had older friends and cousins in the same school so of course when I walked in the lunch room I met up with them. I was explaining to them how much of a change this school was from elementary with smiles. I couldn't stop talking about the girls. My friends and cousins immediately gave me the run-down of everything that was going on in the lunch room.

My cousin looked me in my eyes and said, "It's a jungle in here!"

He explained certain politics in a way that only he could explain! And he was absolutely right. It was a jungle, mixed with a popularity contest. I was like a sponge. Soaking in all the information that I could and learning things as I went. I was smart enough to know that my cousin and friends didn't know everything because they only spent about two or three hours at school a day. I only saw my cousin and his squad at lunch and in the mornings anyway. I saw him in the mornings of course because we lived together and he gave me a ride. But then he would just disappear! Sometimes he just dropped me off and kept it moving. Like, didn't even come in the school. After about a month or two of the way they acted, I had pretty much made my own assessment of what was going on. I looked up to him so much because of how much respect he got from the others around him. He never was the type to have the good grades in school but he always had money! That intrigued the hell out of me. I mean I was at that age where I was questioning everything. I had to catch on to things just as quick as my peers.

My teachers were harder on me because they thought that I was given special privileges since I was skipped. I basically had to prove myself in my every move. I accepted everything as a personal challenge. This made me study harder on my own just to prove that I belonged. I also wanted to be a part of the cool crowd. Popularity was key in school so I figured the best way for me to get noticed outside or being the smart kid was to try out for the basketball team.

Tryouts were a month away and I knew the best way to get prepared for it was to play against my competition. I knew that a lot of the players on the team had gym during 4th period. That was the same period my cousin had gym so I used that as my excuse to go check things out. I decided to skip class one day and I went to the gym. I told my cousin that I didn't feel good and since he was a senior, he could pretty much leave after 4th period. It was like a half of day for him. I told him I didn't want to wait in the office and asked if I could just stay in there with him till it was over. Besides, it was gym which meant an easy A!

Nobody took gym serious but I had a plan.

Fourth period was the longest period of the day because lunch ran around that time. It was two and a half hours with the gym class actually being the last lunch period. It was more than enough time for me to play basketball with the team. I couldn't just jump into the situation fast so I was smart about it. I told my cousin that we should shoot for money! He looked at me and laughed. He laughed because he was terrible in basketball but the fact that he was a big time gambler, I knew he would do it anyway. After about 10 shots and losing $50, he decided to call one of his friends up to shoot for him against me. Twenty minutes passed and I had a quick $200 in my pocket! That was the quickest money I had ever made in my life.

We started to create a crowd because in that gym period, it was all politics going on. Some guy in the crowd wanted to shoot against me and my cousin immediately put him to the challenge. His name was 'Smoke'. I guess they called him that because of his dark ass complexion. Who knows! But he was the starting point guard on the varsity basketball team. My plan had worked and a lot quicker than I thought! I told my cousin I didn't want to shoot anymore but that I'd rather play one-on-one. He looked at me and pulled me to the side.

He asked me, "Are you sure!?"

I looked back at him with a still face. "Hell yeah! And I'll bet my own money!"

In my head, I already won close to $300 so I didn't have anything to lose, but I could gain the respect of not only the starting point guard on the team, but also the whole crowd of people watching us about to play. Smoke immediately accepted the challenge but I could tell he was nervous. I could literally see it in his eyes. And I knew why. See, if he lost to a kid that was literally four grades behind him, not only would it hurt his pride, but it would also hurt his reputation. And in highschool, reputation is everything. After a long and grueling 25 minute one-on-one game, Smoke beat me 12 to 10! I was out $50 and had lost the match. It didn't bother me at all that I lost because I knew that I was probably going to lose the match going into the situation. But I also knew that I had won the war because since the game was so close, I was going to be the talk of the school.

There I was, a skipped 8th grader playing the starting point guard of the school and almost winning! It was the talk of the whole lunch period. I actually surprised myself because I didn't know how good I was until that moment. And I loved the fact that the whole school was talking about how I almost won the game. I never was the type who wanted or needed extra attention, but I knew that it would get back to the head coach of the basketball team.

From then on, after school, the first thing I did was work on my basketball skills. My aunt and uncle worked hard but weren't able to get us certain things that other people had. My uncle was a body mechanic and my aunt worked from home. She took care of foster kids so our house was always full. At one point, there were 10 of us in the same house. I called my foster family my extended family. Since my brothers and I had been through the same thing a couple years earlier, I understood and accepted it with no problem. My aunt knew the importance of keeping a family together so she would never just take one sibling. If they had a family in a group home, then she would take all the brothers and sisters to keep them together. Some stayed with us for years, some stayed with us for only a couple of months. There never was a dull moment in our household. We all were pretty close in age, just a couple years apart. So for me, it was easy to get all my family to help me play basketball. I always played with people older than me and would make my younger siblings play me two-on-one. I watched the games that I could on TV and tried to emulate those same moves whenever I played. It was like I had a photographic memory. I literally studied the game as much as I studied for school. I would go to the library and get books and magazines to learn more about the game. It quickly transitioned from a hobby of mine to a passion.

Tryouts were a week away and I was so anxious that I would go to sleep early just so the days would end faster. My grades were up to par and I had all the confidence in the world. I had proven teachers wrong by showing them that I belonged exactly where I was. It was a Friday and we had just gotten our first report cards. I had 3 A's and 3 B's. That was pretty solid for a kid who skipped a grade. I rushed home after school to show my aunt my grades because I knew that it would make her proud. When I walked through the door, my aunt was on the phone giving me the signal to basically leave her alone because she was on an important phone call. So I changed my clothes and I went straight to the backyard and started playing basketball.

About 30 minutes later, she called me and my brothers in the house. When we walked in, she had tears in her eyes and I immediately knew that there was a problem. She had this look on her face that I will never forget! She couldn't even get the words out because she was crying so hard. We all went over to console her and try to get her to talk but she wouldn't. All she could do was pray. So I got on my knees right beside her and just closed my eyes. We all did. It wasn't until the end of her prayer that we actually knew what was going on. My Aunt Sherell, the 2nd oldest of my aunts had just passed away. I didn't know how to react. I was speechless. She was actually my favorite aunt of them all. My aunt who took care of me was more like a mother to me so I never looked at her as just my 'auntie'. I was heartbroken but I knew that it hurt her a lot more than it hurt me. I didn't understand death at the time, so I took me forever to cope. There was just a cold silence in our home for the next couple of hours. I didn't know what to do so I did the only thing in the world that could take my mind off of the situation. I went outside and played basketball! I shot the ball until it was dark outside. Then it started to rain. I didn't even realize it was raining. All I could think about was the memories I had of my aunt. I thought the rain was my Aunt Sherell crying down from heaven and it actually made sense to me. My uncle came home from work that night and saw me playing basketball in the backyard in the rain. I mean it was lightning and thundering but all I could think about was my aunt Sherell..

My Aunt Sherell was the cool one out of all her sisters. She was the one that would always get us the cool clothes for school and the best presents for our birthdays. I knew that she would've taken me and my brothers in just as quick as her sister did. She didn't have any kids so she literally spoiled us.

We left that Sunday to head to New York where she was going to be buried. Her funeral was later on that week.

It was a deep emotional time for my brothers and me because that was the first time we saw our mother since they took us from her. She looked exactly how I saw her in my dreams. Still young, still beautiful, still everything. It was like seeing a ghost! As soon as she saw us she ran up to us and cried. It was a feeling that I hadn't felt in years! I can't even put into words the instant joy I felt looking at her face. I hated that I had to see her under these circumstances but for about 30 minutes, I forgot the reason we were there.

Things were more awkward then before. It was like this tension in the room between my Aunt and mother that I couldn't describe. Naturally my aunt was a bit jealous of the love and attention we gave to my mother, but I didn't care. I wanted to be with my mother! I noticed little settle jabs my aunt took at my mother, saying things to provoke her. I also noticed small sneaky things my mother would do to try to get under her skin. It was like my mother was using us to make my aunt mad. I didn't like that shit at all. I mean, if it wasn't for my aunt, we would be lost in the system somewhere and more than likely, separated! Eventually they both got into a huge argument right in front of the whole family!! It was terrible. They went at it and talked about each other like they weren't even real sisters. Fighting, name calling, and screaming to the top of their lungs. It hurt so bad, that I just left. I went for a long walk to clear my head. I didn't even go to the wake, because being in the same room as them made me feel some type of way. It was like they wanted us to pick sides and that shit was confusing.

The next day at the funeral, my mother didn't show up. I figured she was going to be late, but she didn't show up at all. Nobody knew where she was. After the ceremony, when we went home, there was a letter from my mother there. After my aunt read it, she gave it to me. My mother had disappeared once again! That shit hurt me to my soul! In my eyes, I thought my mother was coming back into my life to get me and my brothers but I was wrong. I was terribly wrong. All the things my aunt use to say to me about my mother started making sense. Once again, she was running away from her responsibilities.

That situation put me in a dark place. I was depressed. When I finally got back to school, I had missed basketball tryouts. Basketball was the furthest thing on my mind at the time, so I didn't care at all. After seeing me play in gym class a couple of times, the head basketball coach came up to me and asked me why I didn't try out for the team. My answer was nonchalant and direct. "Because I got other shit to worry about back home!" As I walked off, I immediately regretted saying that.

Time went on and I continued on as a regular student. School was starting to bore me. It was becoming redundant. Everything was the same all day every day. School and home, school and home. I needed something else to motivate me. I decided to play AAU basketball. This was basically summer basketball, but it was better than playing in high school because you get to travel and play competition from all around the country. Since I was in High school, I started off playing against my peers in my class. I was doing great and holding my own with them, but when college coaches and other high school coaches got the information back that I was actually 2 years younger than the competition, they made a big deal out of it! I never saw a need for me to play down with my age, so I continued on playing with my class and not my age group. I was getting better and better and I knew the only way to be the best was to continue to play against competition better than me. The word spread fast. I started to even receive college letters of interest at my high school. This made the high school coach feel some type of way because I wasn't playing for his team. The assistant coach at my high school would tell me about the college letters that would come to the athletic department that the head coach never would give me. Eventually, the assistant coach started to give me the letters. This made me not want to play for this guy even more.

III

The following year, I thought about transferring schools, but I didn't want to make the wrong decision. I had my full support cast here. Everybody knew my older cousin and I had made a name for myself. So I was skeptical about leaving, but I did want to play.

It was an average night. We were hungry and my aunt wanted me to go to the grocery store for her. She gave me the list and her car keys and told me to be careful. As I was walking out of the house and starting the car up, I noticed that the car was empty. Instead of asking for gas, I asked my older cousin could I drive his car. He was hesitant at first, but eventually gave me the keys when I told him where I was going. I thought he was joking until he actually gave me his keys. My cousin was selfish as hell with his stuff. He wouldn't even let me borrow his clothes, so I was totally surprised when he actually let me drive his brand new Cadillac. Before I left the house, I had a gut feeling that I should just take my aunts keys, but I went against it. I ignored those senses and took the car anyway. I ended up taking the long way to the grocery store of course. I was just excited to be driving. I didn't have nothing but a learners permit so this was definitely a big deal for me. When I got to the grocery store, I picked up everything off the list and rushed back to the car. I even parked in the handicap parking space just to show off. Besides, I knew I wasn't going to be in the store long. I took the long way home again of course, but this time, I was more confident and even had the music playing loud as fuck. After about 5 minutes, I saw the cop lights behind me and I almost pissed in my pants! I knew I was legit with my license and stuff, but I was in my brother's car. The first thing the cop noticed when he approached the car was that it smelled like weed. He asked, "License and registration." I proceeded to give it to him and he walked back to his car. Before he came back to the car, another cop car pulled up. I had no idea why the other cop car came, but I figured it was because he was just around and saw us and not because the other car called for backup. They both came back to the car and asked me to step out. After sitting me down un-handcuffed on the curb, they asked me could they search the car. When I asked why, the officer replied, "We have probable cause!" I guess it was the smell of the weed in the car. One officer stayed with me asking a bunch of questions, while the other officer searched the car. Then they switched turns. Nothing was found. I figured it was just a routine stop until a third cop pulled up. This cop hopped out with a big ass German Shepard. At this point, I'm beyond scared and don't know what to do. I thought about running initially, but I knew I was innocent so I stuck it out. The dog ran into the trunk and they immediately put me in handcuffs! As they were walking me into the police car, I turned around and saw the officers pulling drugs out of the speaker box from the trunk. I was so scared and shocked that I didn't say a single word. When they took me to jail, they took me to the adult jail. The seriousness of the charges brought against me caused them to forgo juvenile and put me in the big jail. I went through the process booking and then later taken into the interrogation room. In the interrogation room I didn't say much. I only gave them one word answers. I was still in shock and fear but I was smart enough to know that saying anything without a lawyer present would be incriminating. Here I was, a 15 year old kid in a adult jail being interrogated by two loser ass cops about a situation that I didn't know a damn thing about. I was so scared and nervous that I literally started laughing. The more they asked, the more I was determined not to say anything. After about 3 hours of pointless interrogation, the detectives decided to let me out of the interrogation room. On the way out I asked, "When do I get a phone call?" The officer replied, "When we figure out how to lock your fucking brother up!"

Days turned into weeks, and weeks eventually turned into months. My parents didn't have enough money to get the fancy lawyers, but I was innocent so I thought that things would just sort themselves out. I cried almost every day in my cell, but eventually couldn't cry anymore. During one of my visitations, my aunt told me that sometimes in this world, bad things happen to good people. That really hit me when she said that. Especially since I was spending my 16th birthday in a fucking jail cell.

My AAU basketball coach was aware of my situation. He was the secretary of the state so he helped me out as much as he could. He got me a lawyer and also helped speed up my trial process. After 4 months of not knowing my fate, I finally had a trial date. I was found guilty and my heart dropped.

Going to prison was the worst thing that ever happened to me. It gave me a different outlook on the world. I was already on edge and felt like the world had pushed me. It made me numb and emotionless! Anger was only about 15 percent of how I actually felt. The only word to describe how I felt: UNFORGIVING! I lost hope. I lost faith. There I was, a 16 year old kid in a state prison with murderers, robbers, rapists and all types of other crazy motherfuckers who made my 24 month sentence seem like a vacation. Naturally, I was scared as hell and nervous, but after chopping it up with my cellmate, my fears immediately changed.

My cellmate was a Mexican dude, 25-26 years old, clean cut, and way too damn comfortable to be in jail. We'll just call him Knowledge for the sake of this story. Knowledge was on his eighth year of a 12 year sentence, so he knew the ropes, to say the least. He knew exactly what I was going through because he was locked up right around my same age. He was only 18 when he first came through those same doors. I didn't bother to ask why he was in prison. I figured if he wanted me to know, then he'd tell me. The only reason I knew how much time he had was because of the artwork drawn all over the cell. I knew this nigga was different because instead of having regular calendars, he had different variations of the Mayan Calendar all over the cell and deep and dark paintings. It looked like he was getting ready for an art gallery. I was specifically drawn to this carving on the wall which was a mask and a calendar.

As I rubbed the grooves and curves in the wall, I thought to myself how long it took to create this image.

While I was tranced in this image, I heard Knowledge mutter a few words. "One more day! One more fucking day!"

I asked Knowledge what that meant and he told me he only had 1 more day to do for a 12 year sentence.

"Damn my nigga, you only got one more day?" I said.

"You only do two days when you're incarcerated, the day you come in and the day you get out!"

After he said that, the carvings in the wall made sense. I was never in to art but you could see and feel the pain in the eyes of the faces he created. It was like the walls came alive.

"I get the feeling you been in here for a long time. This my first go round. Any advice?" "Make it your last!" Knowledge insisted.

That was the realest answer I could have received, short and sweet! But that's how Knowledge was. He would never say too much and never say too little. It was like he would let you figure things out, but gave you little clues here and there. Always dropping knowledge.

"Everything is a routine in prison. Get you a routine and stick to it! Time passes whether you think about it or not. If you stay active in your routines, time passes faster. Never date the days. It's either night time or day time to me. And right now, they're about to pop these locks for breakfast. Oh. And the best teacher is experience. Here comes State Prison 101 now!"

All I kept thinking was this nigga Knowledge must have been institutionalized because 20 seconds after he said that, the guards popped the locks on the cells for breakfast. I almost pissed on myself when those locks popped on me for the first time. I knew this was it. I was hesitant to walk out but I didn't want to let Knowledge get too far ahead of me. Shit, he was all I knew so far and he seemed cool. When I walked out of my cell, the first thing I noticed was how many people were locked up. There were inmates everywhere. You know when you kick over an anthill and the ants come pouring out by the thousands? Like that! As soon as those locks popped, that's exactly how prison looked. There were all races, all shapes and sizes in prison.

Some inmates looked all kinds of guilty and others like they didn't belong there. I was a new face on the block so I knew everything I did was under a microscope by the other inmates. I was being judged harder than ever, from my mannerisms to the people with whom I associated. I didn't want to seem weak like I couldn't stand on my own so I kept my distance walking from the tier to the cafeteria. At the same time, I didn't want to stand out alone, so I sat by Knowledge in the cafeteria. This way, if anybody was wondering who the new kid was, they knew who to ask! At that point I was starving. I didn't eat the day before because of all the transferring and processing. But there was no fucking way that I was going to eat that bullshit prison food though. My breakfast food looked like a yogurt and oatmeal concoction. I can't even explain the grimy texture. I honestly wouldn't have fed that shit to my dog.

As I picked up the oatmeal-yogurt bullshit to smell it, Knowledge said to me, "Welcome to the pin!"

We laughed and that's when I noticed he wasn't eating. He traded his breakfast for favors and juice. That's when he broke down some of the politics of prison to me.

After we ate, people went every which way to complete their different programs for the day. Some had actual jobs, GED programs and even college classes to attend. You could learn a trade or even teach a class. Every inmate was participating in some program in order to make the time go by faster. They also gave you a lesser sentence once you finished certain programs or had a job. A lot of inmates worked because they didn't have family on the outside to put money on their books. And I realized quickly that having money on your books for commissary was important, especially after seeing how terrible the food could be at breakfast.

They put me in a GED program but that was too slow for me. I already knew what they were teaching but I also didn't want to seem like a know-it-all. So I did what I still do best: I sat back and observed. After about a week, I was a lot more comfortable in my environment. All the loud noises, chaos, and rumbling that I heard when I first got in started becoming clearer. I could understand the conversations and lingo better now. I went from being scared and nervous to calm and aware. After about a month, everything became routine to me. I didn't have the type of family on the outside that could keep money on my books and I didn't want them worried about me either. I had to come up with my own hustle to get money in there. I was super observant.

But my couple of months couldn't compare to the eight + years Knowledge had. He knew how everything worked and everybody knew him. Knowledge was a barber in prison. This allowed him more free-time out of the cell and it was a way to communicate with the other inmates. This nigga cut everybody's hair: Whites, Blacks, Hispanics, and Asians. Everybody.

He also had a nice weed plug through his older brother who did five years in prison. I never asked how he smuggled it; I just knew that he was connected with the right people. Knowledge being so connected was the security I needed to back my idea. The penitentiary barbershop wasn't too much different from barbershops on the street. People discussed politics from government affairs to current events on the streets. In prison, it's gang politics. That was when I started to weigh my prison hustle options. I didn't want to join a gang because they always had too much shit going on. I wanted to basically fly under the radar and then go home. I kept thinking about what Knowledge said to me. 'Two days. The day you come in and the day you leave!'

Getting involved in the drug trade was too much of a risk. I was a small fish in a big ocean in there. Running the pros and cons of every possible operation through my head, I had an epiphany. The thing everybody in the pin had in common was sports. And I was good with numbers. So after a week of formulation and thought, I sat down with Knowledge to tell him my plan.

"Aye, how much money you make a month, my nigga?! The reason I ask is because we living together. So naturally, I know a couple of your hustles. I know you cut hair and I also know you got the weed grind going. Business must be pretty good because you don't want a thing in here. But how much money you really making?"

"I make enough to take care of myself and my obligations on the street," he said. That's when I told him my plan.

"Every inmate in here watches sports and we all gamble. Whether it's actual money or something traded of value. I'm pretty good with numbers so I want to create a gambling sports line with a $1,000 credit line. That's where you come in at. I don't have a stack. So I need you to be the house, or the bank. It's easier if you be the bank 'cause if there's a problem with the payout, well, it's easier to lose to a grown ass man than to a 17 year old kid. The house is incentivized to minimize payouts. I do this by offsetting each side of the bet against the other while making money off the rake in the middle. The closer they get to even odds, the higher the rake will be with respect to any discrepancy to one side or the other of the line."

Knowledge looked a little puzzled. "Sooooo, what you saying?" He asked.

"Basically we want to take in a mixture of bets at odds that ensure they will make money no matter who wins! I'm creating the odds, but it's more about eliminating risks. You can get the word out quicker and more discrete because you work in the barbershop. Your weed grind will also bring in more gamblers who you already have an established relationship with. I'm the brains behind the operation. I just need you to be the muscle and the bank. You can't take on too many bets though, because it's only $1,000 in the pot and if somehow everybody wins, well, we have to pay everybody," I explained.

Knowledge agreed and we were in business. It took a whole week to come up with the proper numbers, but once I got it, we were good. It was like clockwork. I set the sports line for all football and basketball games. Every week we made nearly $500 after paying out the people who won. It was genius! We kept it small with the bank pot only being $1,000 so we wouldn't have too much attention drawn to us. But as we expected, business eventually grew. We always split the money 50/50 but as business grew, we had to expand the pot. I didn't want to expand because adding more money opened up the system for more bets. More bets meant having to deal with more people and more money in the pot that I didn't have. Knowledge wanted to set the pot to $10,000. I didn't agree with him at all. He obviously had the money and was looking to expand.

"If we upped the pot 10 times, then that $500 a week can be $5,000 a week.

That's easy math young fella," Knowledge said to me.

"True," I argued. "But we also would have to take 10 times as many bets. That's a lot of traffic, making it damn near impossible to stay low-key. Plus, I'm doing these numbers myself, so it's going to take a longer period of time to do."

"Well teach me how to do the numbers, King! It can't be that hard."

"You right. It's actually not that hard once you know the algorithm, but it's fucking time consuming! I'll be a damn fool if I showed you how to do the equation because who's to say that you won't run off and do the sports line yourself!? In this business partnership, you are the bank. But I also like the leverage I have being able to set the line. If you feel like you can cover that

$10,000 bank, then I'll set the line. But we both know… it's only a matter of time."

After a couple days of preparation, I set the sports line with the bank being 10k. This immediately involved more inmates because I had to get enough bets out to win on both sides. But the more people got involved, the more personalities we encountered. I was hesitant to do it, but I went against my better judgment. Things were beautiful and going as planned for about three weeks.

I guess the big dogs in prison started hearing about the money we were making and wanted in on the action. They had to hear about the ring from Knowledge because even though we were getting paid, my routine stayed the same: same lunch, same programs, and same time. I remained super low-key, still doing everything the same even though I was making $2,500 a week now. In prison, with the have-nots, that $2,500 a week was like $25,000 a week on the street. So my pockets changed but nothing else did.

One day, three of the biggest fucking Mexicans I had ever seen in my life unexpectedly walked in my cell. I honestly don't even know how the hell they fit in that little ass cell but they caught me at the right time.

This was prison, you could never get comfortable! I was literally sharpening a knife against the wall that I made from a piece of metal off the toilet. I grabbed it and jumped up off the floor!

"What's popping?" I said to the Mexicans. "Can I help you? Knowledge ain't here right now."

These two big motherfuckers didn't say a word. They looked around and then just walked out. I'm assuming they went to pay Knowledge a visit at the barbershop because he had a different attitude when he came back in to the cell.

I told him what happened.

"Aye man, a couple of ya uncles and ancestors came in here looking for you! I was about to give one of them niggas another permanent tattoo but they walked off. What was that about?"

"Well, I'm afraid what you didn't want to happen is about to happen!"

"What's that mean?" I asked with concern.

"Let's just say I owed some money and paid it off a lot quicker than expected. They wanted to know how and I had to tell them. More than likely he knew anyway because that's just how prison works. He's a big dog. A shot caller. Leader of my set. Shit, if I woulda lied to him, then we both woulda died tonight! So I told him the truth!"

I shook my head.

"You know for a nigga named Knowledge, you sure did some dumbass shit!"

"Yeah I told him about the sports line but I couldn't tell him exactly how that shit works! Only you can do that! So I presented it in a way that is beneficial to him with us being assets," he explained.

"Us!?" I yelled.

"Yeah! US motherfucker! You the brain, I'm the bank. Nothing changed, the bank is just higher. Instead of 10 racks, it's 50 now. It's prison, King, prison politics! I don't know how that algorithm shit works, so I don't know how much time you need. But I seriously suggest you get on it.

Because these orders are definitely coming from the no fuck around gang!"

"Well I need to talk to him then. Because for a $50,000 odd algorithm, to plan a minimum payout is going to take me some time. I need to explain this face to face so that I can show him what I mean. And like you said, you don't know the algorithm. So I need you to schedule that face to face for me."

Knowledge agreed. You see, Knowledge was part of a set that I didn't know shit about. And I'm not the type to ask too many questions. We had been locked up almost six months and I never even asked him why he was in prison. There I was, about to sit down with his big homie. I didn't know who that Latin motherfucker was on the streets, but in prison, this nigga was the mother fucking man! El Capo for real! I had to be brought to him because he wasn't even housed in the same unit as us. Two Mexican guards actually had to escort me to him. I walked in nervous and in awe! His cell looked like a business office. As we sat down and talked, I humbly said my piece.

"I came up with an algorithm that works basically playing the odds. I'm pretty good with numbers so it's hard to explain. It's my idea and Knowledge is my financial backing. I know you want to up the bank and I'm fine with that; I'll continue to come up with the sports line for you. All I ask is that you don't involve me with any percentage of the money. I'll do it for free. Just make sure it's $500 a month on my book for commissary because I don't eat the shit in here. I ain't sure 'bout what you and Knowledge worked out and that's none of my business, but this is my only request."

El Capo was a man of few words in that meeting. There were a lot of head nods and hand gestures. He agreed and shook my hand firmly. As he shook my hand, he stared in my eyes as if he was reading me. Then he stood up.

"Why no money for you? I can't wrap my head around the fact that you would give up your percentage for snacks and shit. So I agree with the deal because it's more money for me, but you stand to lose almost $40,000 a month. So why!?" He asked.

I sighed. "Well I'm only 17 years old. I wouldn't know what to do with 40 racks on the street, let alone in prison. Shit knowing me, I'd try to pay my way out of here. Twenty four months is a hell of a long time when you innocent. The truth is, I only came up with this idea because I know my family can't afford to put money on my books. That may seem like all the more reason to make the 40 racks, but that's also a lot of attention. And if it's one thing I don't want in prison, it's attention. The bigger the bank, the more bets you can take, causing an unlimited amount of earning potential. And to be honest, Sir, that's something I'm not ready for."

He stood there kind of startled.

"What the fuck are you in for young fella!? What you do?"

I thought about it for a second then took a deep breath. "It ain't about what I did. This is about who I wouldn't tell on. And to be honest, I'd make the same decision again. I guess I'm in here to learn something. The universe doesn't make mistakes."

After about a 15 to 20 minute conversation, El Capo agreed to my terms of the deal and I was off to my cell. I told Knowledge about it when he got back from his work shift, but he already knew. Word spread fast in prison. Real fast.

Business continued to pick up just as I expected. It only took a month before it was "the thing to do." Inmates were actually winning and getting their payouts. As long as there was enough money in the bank to cover the winnings, there were going to be some wins and even bigger losses. Eventually, shit started to spiral out of control. I would even hear the guards and other staff members throughout the prison placing bets. I never said a word about me being the one setting the line; I just played along with it like everybody else. When people asked me about placing a bet, I just told them I didn't gamble. Things were going perfect, almost too perfect, so I felt like it was only a matter of time before it came crashing down. There were certain variables that you could never add to the equation because so many aspects were unknown and unexpected. That's why I didn't want to be the face of the project.

Things started getting violent around the prison: murders, stabbings, and extortions from other inmates who saw or knew about somebody with a winning ticket. The shit got crazy!

Knowledge, El Capo, and I knew not to say a word about the sports line because we knew that if we did, all of that bullshit going on in there would be pinned on us as a result. All the violence just brought on extra attention from the police. Twenty three hour lockdowns and all privileges were taken away from everyone. Even the programs were shut down so nobody could leave their cells. There was literally a war going on outside so I understood the lockdown and felt safer in my damn cell anyway. All sense of time was lost with regular policies, but with the lockdown in place, nobody even knew if it was even day or night. That one hour of free time came randomly throughout the day so we never knew when they were coming to pop the locks. After about a week of being on lockdown, we had a random 3 a.m. shakedown. The warden was looking for weapons and contraband because of all the recent violence. Knowledge and I heard them waking up the inmates next to our cell and he started to panic. He jumped up and started flushing magazine papers down the toilet. He had heroin attached to the papers and didn't want to get caught. I was completely caught by surprise. It was my first shakedown so all I could think about was the knife I made from that metal part of the toilet. By the time my brain registered the guards coming in, they had already found the knife. I was so shook about them finding the knife, I had completely forgotten about the numbers and spreadsheets I had with all the vital and incriminating information from the sports line. They took that and all other contraband they could find in the cell. They took us both straight to the hole: complete isolation from any and everything. The hole is like a separate jail within the prison. The smell alone could break a man. The cell was much smaller, the room was a lot colder, and the silence was so loud that it could drive a man completely insane! I sat in that bitch for two weeks with no sense of time or connection to the outside world. I only knew two weeks had passed because I counted the days through our food. Three meals **a day** and I was on my 42nd meal. There were only about two inches of light that could get into the cell from a small slit in the window.

The warden finally did two full investigation and brought me into his office. The first thing I noticed was how El Capo's cell looked better than the warden's office. I laughed to myself and thought, ain't no way I'm telling on this nigga and he living better than you in here! Warden James questioned me and I told him everything he wanted to know. I told him it was my idea, that I was the brain behind the operation, and I even showed him the algorithm that I used. The only thing I didn't tell him was how I provided the bank. I kept Knowledge's name out of it and wouldn't have told on El Capo if my own life depended on it. When it came to providing the bank supply, I explained it in a way that made sense.

I explained to the warden, "Warden, the inmates paid themselves. I started slow, setting the bets to payout on both sides. And as it grew, the bank grew. The bank was only $150 at first, but I raked in about $300 after the first week. I kept doing this until the bank grew out of my control. I started doing this only to pay for my meals since I don't eat 85 percent of the food y'all serve. Then it spiraled and took on a life of its own. When I saw people dying, getting stabbed and extorted all from something I was doing, I immediately stopped it. Nobody knew I was the brain behind the operation and that's how I wanted it. Me being anonymous was for my own security. If these niggas in here knew it was a kid running the sports line in prison, well, that would've been some attention I wasn't ready for. So I kept it low-key."

Warden James seemed to be more impressed than angry.

Then he asked me, "Where do you see yourself in the next five years?" Short and sweet, I said, "Not in here!"

Warden James sent me back to the hole till he figured out that there was a lot of truth to my story. Then he dug further into my case to try and see why I was in prison in the first place.

He came to the hole to pay me a visit about a week later.

"You know when I first met you, I thought you were full of shit! I didn't believe you were telling the truth but you spoke in a way that intrigued me. So much confidence for such a young fella. Then I thought to myself, *maybe he's taking up for one of his big homies on some gang shit*. So I did a little homework and you're not even gang affiliated. But your celly, now he's another story. I know all about his Mexican tithes. So as I sit here and contemplate on what to do with you, I can't come to a conclusion because I know there's more to this story! Let me see if another week in the hole will refresh your memory!" The warden said threateningly.

I didn't say a word. I just looked at him right in his eyes and shrugged my shoulders. I went back to isolation after the meeting. After about three days of being completely lost, I broke down and started going crazy! My mind started to play tricks on me. The walls seemed to get smaller and the room seemed to spin. I started seeing images out of pure darkness. I tried to sleep the days away because when I was asleep, I wasn't in prison. My dreams were very vivid. Sort of like déjà vu. I woke up more relaxed but drenched in cold sweats. But as time passed, I learned to cope and things became routine again. Even though I was in isolation, prison was easier to deal with that way: just me and my thoughts. I was nearly in the hole for three months before they released me back into population. That shit felt like a whole year. It actually transformed me. I came back looking totally different. I hadn't had a haircut in almost 90 days and I damn sure hadn't combed it. I had a bush nappy blowout! All I did in the hole was sleep, read, pray, eat, and workout. I mean, there was nothing more to do.

The first person I wanted to see was Knowledge, but before I could even get back to the cell, two more big ass guards escorted me back to see El Capo. I walked into his cell office this time without being nervous or scared. I was anxious to see what the fuck he wanted.

As soon as he tried to speak I cut him off, "Man I ain't tell those people a fucking word. I owned up to it and told them it was me, which isn't a lie because this was actually my plan. Of course they knew there was more to the story, but after seeing how stubborn I was, the warden just made me sit in the hole for 90 days. I'm not a snitch. Shit that's the reason I'm even in here!"

El Capo replied, "Yeah I know all about your case. I don't go in to business with people without doing my homework first. I even know things that you don't know. Like I'm sure you don't know that the Feds finally caught up with your brother and he's locked up now getting ready to be sent to a federal prison! Did you know that? Of course not because you been in isolation for the past 90 days. No phone calls, one shower per week, shitty food, no visits. And yet, you kept your mouth shut. I can respect that. I do respect that! It's a sign of strength and mental toughness that a lot of people don't exemplify. You are who you are in this world; You just gotta learn to embrace it. I made more money quicker with you than I did with any of my other businesses in here. And when things got out of hand, you stood tall. I want to repay you. You're a smart kid with a bright future. You have less than a year to do on your bid, so I'm going to get you out of here early!"

I stopped El Capo again, "With all due respect, I'm not sure if I need your type of help. I mean what's meant to be will be, right? I can't afford to do some more illegal shit in here and get more time. I'm not a criminal, I just had to adapt!"

"And that's what I like about you, your willingness to do what it takes. You know why I'm in here?"

"No. I didn't ask because it's none of my business."

"You can do the wrong thing for the right reason. That makes it justifiable. All you need is the right push. Let's just say that I got friends in high places that owe me a favor or two. So I'm going to get you out of here. You just make sure you make the best of it because I'm not gonna be in here forever. And when I get out, we will speak again!"

I didn't take to heart what he said about getting me out of prison, but it was definitely on my mind. I brushed it off because I thought to myself, *how can he get me out of prison but can't get himself out of here.* With a lot on my mind, I went to the barbershop later that day and finally ran into Knowledge.

"What's happening, my nigga? I know I'm good for a free haircut!" We both laughed as I sat down for my cut.

"You look like a real criminal now, King!"

As he cut my hair, we chopped it up and caught up on everything that was going on.

When we got back to the cell, I told him what El Capo said about getting me out early. "Congratulations, my G!"

"What you mean!?" I asked him.

"Well, El Capo isn't the type to say things he doesn't mean. He has a lot of politics in his pocket. He's only in here for tax evasion. They couldn't pin anything else on him. He will be out of here in less than five years. Looks like he took a liking to you."

Later that week, I got a visit from my old basketball coach. He was the secretary of the state and also had some political power. Coach sat down and started talking to me.

"I heard about everything that's going on in here. The warden is my fraternity brother.

How are you holding up?" He asked.

"You're actually the first visit I've gotten since I've been in here. I didn't do what they said I did, my family just didn't have the money to beat the case. I took the plea deal because if I didn't, I would've had to do ten years instead of two. Lose-lose situation. Now I'm just trying to survive to get out of here!" I said.

"What do you want to do when you get out of here, kid?"

I paused for a minute, looked in his eyes and replied, "Coach, I honestly can't think that far ahead. I don't know how… if!... I'm going to make it through the week let alone when I get out. I've seen people get stabbed over honey buns! I watched people lose their life over unpaid bets! I've seen the weak get preyed upon and extorted because they didn't want to take part in gang activities. I watched guards allow inmates to get jumped in their cells and didn't report a thing. I just did 90 days in isolation and the weird part about that experience is that that's the only time I felt safe in here. I haven't had a good night's rest since I been in here. It's a fear that I've adapted and gotten used to. I've been on 23 hours lockdown for the past five months. There are no mirrors. I have to look at myself through the reflection of a fucking potato chip bag! So you have to forgive me if I can't think that far ahead!"

Tears rolled down my eyes as I got up. "Where are you going, son?"

Standing up straight, brushing the tears off my face, I said "Back to the hell hole! I'm not really in the mood for talking anymore. I told my family not to visit me in here because that would only make my time longer. This is my first and last visit. I don't want to be sold any false dreams. So before somebody else lies to me, I'd rather not hear anything!"

I had the guard to take me back to my cell.

My coach returned later that week. As I sat down, he could see the frustration on my face. "Before you say a word and get all bent out of shape, let me say a few things! When you left last week, I put in a few calls and also talked to the warden. I can get you out of here in the next 72 hours but you will be released under my supervision, making me responsible for you. I explained your extraordinary talents to the warden and elaborated how you were just at the wrong place at the wrong time. We put together a plan for you under a strict probation. I told him you were a product of your environment. With a change of scenery, I told him your potential is limitless. El Capo, I'm sure you know who that is, also put in a word for you and the warden agreed to release you early. The only stipulation is that you have to come and live with me. We're also working on getting you into a different school," Coach explained.

"Coach, I don't understand."

"Well I convinced the warden that you were a product of your environment so we want to change your environment. I showed him your transcripts from school so he could see the type of student you were. He saw how you were skipped and told me a story about how good you were with numbers. So you were doing a sports line in prison!? That is fucking genius. This made it easy to convince him of your talents outside of basketball. He agreed that releasing you under my supervision was a great idea. New start, new environment! What do you think?" I was hesitant to respond. I didn't know how to take that news.

"Coach, it's hard for me to get my hopes up. I lost that my first week in here. I'll believe it when it happens!"

IV

Seventy-two hours later, I was being released from prison. On one hand, when I walked out of those prison doors, I felt like a slave. Well, a part of me did. I mean, the only reason I got out early was because my AAU summer league coach was the secretary of the state. On the other hand, I felt like a lion uncaged! I had all this pinned up anger and frustration towards the world and wanted to return the feelings of pain, hurt, and embarrassment I felt each one of those agonizing eight months.

I was conveniently released the same weekend as the AAU tournament. I was free but I still felt controlled. Judge Israel released me under the supervision of my AAU coach with the intention of me not becoming a product of my environment so naturally they switched it up. I had all these negative emotions bottled up and felt like the only way to express myself positively was through basketball. So I channeled all of that anger and decided to dominate the game on all levels! Playing the actual game was my escape, my freedom, my voice, and I had some shit to say! They couldn't control me on the court and I knew that.

The AAU tournament was for three days in North Carolina at UNC called the "Bob Gibbons" tournament. I didn't know much about who Bob was or how big this tournament was but I didn't care. While we were warming up for our first game, I noticed a lot of college coaches in the crowd. We were playing some team from California and they had four of the tallest motherfuckers I had ever seen in my life so I figured the college coaches were there to see them. To me, that was just perfect! They were in the warm up line doing shit that would intimidate any young hooper. I'm talking about dunks you could only do on video games. They eventually had my team's undivided attention because I looked up and my teammates were staring at the California team's warm up line. I walked off the court to sit on the bench with about four minutes to go before tip-off. I sat there expressionless. I don't know what my coach saw in my eyes, but he asked me if I was ok. I was so zoned out that I didn't even hear him.

He touched my shoulder to get my attention. "You ready?!"

I just looked over with no reply. I had nothing to say. It was time to show them. The things I felt and thoughts I was processing couldn't be put into words, only actions. As we walked on the court, I didn't even shake anybody's hand. I was ready. Tip-off came and they of course won the jump ball because of these tall ass players. I immediately stole the ball on the first possession. Then I stole the ball again the very next possession. In the first five possessions, I stole the ball every time. After them catching on to my skills and steals, they immediately called a timeout. In the first three minutes of the game, I had 10 points and 5 steals. But I wasn't happy or content. I wanted more! So I went after it. We ended up winning our first game by 32 points; it was a clear blowout. I didn't have much play time because of the score, but with only 15 minutes of action, I finished with 22 points, 7 steals, and 7 rebounds.

My coaches were proud of me and as we walked out of the gym, I could actually feel college coaches whispering about me. I didn't really pay it any attention because I didn't think a college coach would want a kid who had literally just come home from prison!

To advance to the championship game, we had to win five games; Game two was later that night. As we walked in the gym for the second game, the first thing I noticed was a much bigger crowd. Attendance had at least tripled prior to our first game that morning. I was ready to use that energy to showcase my full potential. I wanted everybody in that crowd to know who I was and the only way to do that was to put on a show! We had the same routine as earlier: stretch, warm-up, then around three minutes before tip-off, sit on the bench and study the other team. This team was a lot smaller than the last. My mind immediately went into attack mode.

After winning the jump ball and scoring our first seven possessions by throwing the ball to the post, they called a timeout. They made some necessary adjustments and switched to a zone defense. They eventually caught up and started winning. Even the crowd was going for them; Everybody loves an underdog. We were down 16 points going into halftime and I was livid!

There were 15 of us in all on the team and coach was playing everyone. He was making full five man subs every five to seven minutes. It was good play for everyone but when you're playing with this tactic, it's hard to get a good team rhythm.

I had a closer relationship with coach than the other players so I wasn't timid to speak up in the locker room.

"Coach! It's 9 of them and it's 15 of us! That makes it hard to get on a rhythm. Then we're a lot bigger team, so our press on defense is being broken easily from all that mixed-matches on the floor. They're over there getting a good sweat in and we keep getting subbed. I think whoever's playing the best should be who you keep on the floor. If it ain't broke, don't fix it! Sir."

"Ok King, who do you suggest I start?"

"Coach whoever has been playing the best. I think you should go back with the same starters, just don't sub so soon."

Coach took my advice and we started the second half. Our first possession, I noticed that they were still in zone. The only way to get them out of that zone was to shoot them out of it. I only had 8 points at the half but I also only took two shots. Up to this point, I had only played a total of nine minutes so I was ready to be extra aggressive. I called out a play to get myself open and shot a corner 3 pointer. As soon as it left my hands, I knew it was good money. It felt so good and I went into a zone, so I called the same play again. The crowd started to get a little quiet and I could feel the momentum shifting. I shifted over defense from a full court press to a half court zone. It was a 3-2 zone with me up top since I was the most aggressive defender. This defense caught them off guard, leading to them making a careless pass. My teammate stole the ball and started a zone one fast break with me running the lane. I signaled up for him to throw me the alley-oop. He threw it up perfectly. I jumped and instead of just dunking the ball, I dunked it backwards right on the defender. The crowd went crazy! It got so loud after that play that I didn't hear the referee blow the whistle indicating a timeout. I was in my zone so I stole the ball and dunked it again. The crowd loved it. The dunk didn't count but I had their wholehearted attention. During the timeout, coach told me that they were going to be looking to double team me so I should look to make the extra pass. We were only down eight points coming out of the timeout but we knew we had them where we wanted them. They continued to play zone and my teammates continued to look for me. I ended up making five 3 pointers that game and finishing with 27 points with 21 minutes of playing time. We also won by 12 points which was the most important thing to me. People from the crowd and players from other teams that were in attendance came up to me and gave me props for my game.

We ordered pizza that night at the hotel while we had a team meeting. During the meeting, coach gave us our schedule for the next day and then told us our rankings during the first day of tournament play. I never knew that they were ranking us because I didn't know or care how big the tournament was. You see, the Bob Gibbons tournament was held annually inviting all of the best high school talent in the country. Over 300 players are elevated and given an overall and player position ranking. From those player rankings, college coaches recruit and offer scholarships. College was still a far-fetched thought to me. I mean, literally one week ago I was in prison and I knew that was the type of information you couldn't keep from a college coach. Who wants a felon on their team?! These were my thoughts so when my coach talked about certain things, I just tuned him out. What did surprise me and catch my attention was my rankings. For a guy who was nowhere on the scene the previous year and after only two games of evaluation, I was ranked overall number 55. My player position ranking was number 5. They had me ranked as a combo guard. I knew I could move up in the rankings as time went on, but I more so wanted to win the tournament. Before I fell sleep that night, I prayed for the first time in over a year. I always believed in God, I just didn't want to talk to him with so much anger and hatred in my heart.

"Father," I began to pray. "I want to thank you for life! I want to thank you for the opportunity to showcase my God given abilities in front of the right people today. I pray that they see me for who I am, and not what I been through. It's hard for me to express my feelings through words so I ask that you just listen to my heart. Work for me in the supernatural. And that you open doors for me that no man can close! Amen."

I woke up the next morning feeling like a new man! I felt happy and less angry than the day before. Like a weight had been lifted. We had two games again that day; The first was at 12:30 p.m. and the second was at 8:30 p.m. That was the prime time game. We had the same routine as the day before so things went a lot faster today. As we walked in the gym, I could literally feel the coaches talking about me. "Pay attention to Brady," I heard in the background.

The negative thoughts that I had were ones of embarrassment. I felt like when people looked at me, they looked at me as an ex-convict. So once I heard a coach say something positive about me, I knew that was all the support I needed. After stretching and warming up, I made my way towards the bench with three minutes till tip off as usual. I looked into the crowd and made eye contact with three different coaches on three separate teams.

The first coach had on all of his UGA apparel so I assumed he was a representative of that university. We made eye contact for about two seconds then he nodded his head and tapped his clipboard. The second coach was a younger guy. He represented the Cincinnati Bear Cats. He pointed directly at me with his right hand and with his left hand, waved two fingers back and forth to his eyes and mine signaling that he was watching me. The last coach was the boldest of the three. Seeing as how no coach or representatives were allowed to talk to the players, him grabbing my shoulder and then saying, "We're coming to get you," probably would have gotten him in trouble so I won't mention the school he represented.

I had supreme confidence at the start of the first game. After seeing those caliber coaches go out of their way to acknowledge me, I wanted to exceed whatever expectations they had of me. I knew my coach wanted all of us to play so we all could get the exposure to those college coaches; I had a plan to get us all involved. Our very first possession, I threw an alley-oop from our special play followed by a quick steal out of our press and an around the back pass. I was going out of my way to make the pass, literally spoon feeding my teammates. I had 12 assists before I even took a shot. When coach went to make his rotation with the subs, he left me in the game because I was in such a good rhythm. My teammates were hitting every shot I passed to them. I don't know how the stars were aligned that day, but I finished the game with 12 points, 19 assists, 7 rebounds, 4 steals, and 2 blocks. The most impressive part was that I did it in only 23 minutes of playing time.

After the game, we had to leave my coach there because he was bombarded with other coaches and questions. The rest of the team left to go eat at Golden Corral. Everyone was hype because we all played so well. We just talked about how our rankings were going to go up. It was all about the rankings to them. I just wanted to get a scholarship to go to college. Something that was a façade a week ago was so obtainable now.

We met back up with coach at the gym a couple hours before our big night primetime game. We were all sitting together watching the current game when all of a sudden coach called me out of the crowd. As he spoke to me, I could hear the excitement and sincerity in his voice.

"King, as of right now, you're considered one of the top 10 players in the country. You could arguably be in the top five but they don't know whether to rank you as a point guard or a shooting guard. You have what's called a good problem. There are over 30 top colleges in the country who are ready to offer you a scholarship."

I stuttered, "So uh, what's the problem coach?" He put his hand on my shoulder.

"The problem is picking the right school! See picking the right school is like picking the right woman to spend the rest of your life with. Take your time and pray for discernment."

I replied, "Coach, I'll cross that bridge when I come to it. Right now, we just want to take the championship back home!"

He went on to say how he discussed my situation with some of the top schools and they weren't threatened by the fact I was just in prison. They did offer to send me to a prep school, though. That way, I could get properly prepared for college and also play against some of the other top talent in the country.

When I initially heard about the prep school setup, it pissed me off! It pissed me off because I immediately equated it to prison. I figured I'd be in a dumb ass uniform just like prison and have those stagnant and monotonous routines again. Overall, my thoughts were just negative on the idea of the whole prep school thing. Then I thought about where I came from and where I was trying to be. I'm bad about wearing my emotions on my sleeve, but I became good at channeling that energy into positive things. I didn't speak before the game, I didn't have to; My emotions were all over my face.

My teammates kept asking if I was ok. I was in my thoughts so I just responded with a head nod or a short, one word reply. As it neared game time with about three minutes left to warm up, I walked over to the bench as always. Coach was extra excited for a number of reasons. He tried to get me to share his enthusiasm but I just couldn't get on his level of optimism. I told him exactly what I had on my mind about the whole prep school proposal.

As usual, coach had some optimistic words to say.

"I don't know how much faith you have, but God doesn't make mistakes, son. If I didn't believe you were innocent then, I wouldn't have fought to get you out of jail. But even with my efforts, it was nobody but God who gave you this second chance and opportunity to change your future! Don't block your blessings with a negative attitude! There are four players on that other team who all go to a prep school, three who ranked higher than you. We got the primetime game and the bright lights are on. Look around, kid! This could all be taken away from you tomorrow. You should know that first hand after all you've been through."

Then he just walked off. He always knew what provoked me and his words did just that. Before the game even started, I was walking on the court getting ready for the jump ball. After all that shit coach just said, the only thing that registered on my brain was the fact that there were three players on the court who thought they were better than me. Three players who ranked higher than me. I wanted to make sure everyone at that tournament knew the difference between them and me. That primetime game was the perfect platform. Regularly, all the games were played on the side courts but this was primetime. We played on the same full court that UNC played their games, making the setting on the court like a real college game.

Things were different this game. It was apparent we were in for a long night from the quick 24-8 lead the other team had over us. They trapped me all over the court, forcing my teammates to make all the plays. I wasn't so effective on offense. After a couple of timeouts, I knew I had to restructure my plans to be effective another way. They forced me to turn the ball over two quick times and I was so fucking frustrated. Coach took me out of the game. As I sat on the bench impatiently, the game started to even out. I sat there watching my team start playing great. While I was ecstatic and thankful we were getting our shit together and coming back, questions, doubts, and negative thoughts rushed my head.

Damn, is it me!? I thought to myself.

I snapped out of it quickly though. Right before coach put me back in, he said something that I will keep with me forever. "You're not playing bad offensively. They're making sure you don't dictate the game. There's more to the game than just scoring, son! And there is no such thing as a bad day on defense."

As usual, he was right. I knew that they were going to keep me out of the game from an offensive standpoint. So I knew I had to separate myself by doing everything else. When I stepped back on the court, I was determined to get every rebound, every steal, and every loose ball. I figured this would help the team because if I wasn't looking to score, then they wouldn't be looking for me to score. This allowed me to roam and get rebounds. I gave us an immediate spark off the bench, grabbing five quick rebounds and getting two quick steals. I was hustling my ass off, in my own way. I grabbed every defensive rebound high above the rim and tapped it on the backboard before my feet hit the ground.

After every tap, I would belt out, "My boards!"

Verbally, I was our defensive anchor. You could hear me yelling out defenses and orchestrating our plays on offense. I was the El Capo of my team. The leader of my set. The shot real life caller. I was the leader and my team followed suit. We eventually went into overtime and I knew... this was my time to shine. I had 4 points, 11 rebounds, 7 assists, and 4 steals going into overtime so they weren't looking for me to score. All of the double teaming tired them out and we started hitting all those shots we had been missing. As overtime started, I noticed I was in single man-to-man coverage. That was my opportunity to help us offensively. I called an isolation play and got two quick 3 pointers. Then I drove to the basket and got a quick layup and a foul. Momentum shifted our way and we pulled out a victory!

We celebrated on the court like we had already won the championship. I was so happy. We had another game but it didn't matter at that point. Fact is, they were the better team but we had more heart. We literally imposed our will on them in front of everybody who was important in the college world. There were a couple of the top prep school programs in the stands and they were all interested in me. They wanted to pair me up with the players I just went up against. After the performance we just put on, I couldn't blame them.

Coach talked to me later that night more in depth about the prep school situation and it made more sense. They were trying to put together a super team on the prep circuit with all the top recruits. That was going to create an elite frenzy because the top colleges had commitments from every player except for one other guy and me. Colleges didn't have a commitment from me because of my incarceration and I was just coming on the scene. Colleges didn't have a commitment from this other guy because he was 7ft tall and trying to figure out if he wanted to go to college or straight to the NBA. I weighed the pros and cons of the situation and asked if I could at least wait till after the tournament to make a decision. He agreed.

That night I couldn't sleep. I felt like I was in this ambiguous dream. There I was, a week out of prison and so much of my life was already changing. All of my teammates were asleep but I was still in shock about the freedom that I had just to walk in and out of the hotel door at will.

I decided to get up and walk around the halls of the hotel. It was almost 4am as I was walking around. The first person I saw was the number one player in the world, the 7 footer who couldn't decide on college or the NBA. We sat and talked for about an hour. He was pretty cool and down to earth.

He wasn't hesitant to tell me why he was up at that time of night roaming the halls like I was, "My mother is locked up right now and this is usually when they wake her up. I'm waiting on her call so we can pray together."

"That's dope. Y'all do that every day?"

He shrugged. "Nah, just three nights out the week. Why are you up?" I just smirked.

"What's funny?" He asked.

"Well, I actually just got out of prison earlier this week. I did about one year of a two year sentence and I'm out right now on special probation. I was released under the supervision of my AAU coach who is also the Secretary of the State. I've been out about a week now."

He just looked at me. He didn't know how to respond. I said it so casually and nonchalant that he didn't even know if I was serious or not.

"Shit, I'm just glad I can open and close the doors without handcuffs on and a guard!"

He saw the look in my eyes and his tone changed; He started to realize I wasn't bullshitting.

"Damn bruh, you for real huh?" He asked.

"I don't even know people to play like that, my nigga! But it's not a big deal, I hear you thinking about making that jump to the NBA."

He humbly replied, "Yeah, but I ain't sure yet. I'm going to this prep school here in North Carolina and Imma decide at the end of the season."

I took a liking to him because I could see a lot of my situation in him. Five minutes ago he didn't think I was serious about the prison thing because of how nonchalant I said it, but there he was using the same nonjudgmental tone. It was an effortless and genuine conversation. Being around so many different personalities in prison, I learned to pick up on vibes so I could read this dude pretty well. He eventually got on the phone with his mother and walked off. As we parted ways, I couldn't help but to think about my mother. That shit immediately changed my mood. I got so caught up in my thoughts that I just sat in the hallway lobby thinking. After about 30 to 45 minutes of daydreaming, I snapped out of it.

I walked toward my room and the big fella stopped me, "Aye bruh, thank God. It could always be worse!"

It was the championship game day and I didn't sleep at all the night before. I was a little tired but still riding that emotional wave from the previous night's win and the overwhelming reception of me. We had to play Omarion, the big fella from last night who was the number one player in the country, and his team. He clearly was a man among boys. Standing 7 foot and weighing 255 pounds, all I could think was *this motherfucker ain't 17 years old, this old man done been here before.* I know I saw him the night before but that was in sweats and flip flops. This dude looked like he grew a couple inches and put on 15 more pounds since last night. It was crazy watching him play. Nobody his size could move as fast as he could and nobody as fast as him was his size! It was a pure mix match and a nightmare for any defender. I could clearly see why he was the number one player overall in high school. Not just for our graduating class, but for all high school and college players. He was the number one prospect in the world. My coach told me that he was going to be the number one pick in the NBA draft for the next five years. We hadn't even started our senior year yet.

Later into the game at the half, he had 22 points and 22 rebounds with little effort against us. Eighteen of those points were dunks! Not just any dunks though; I mean damn near break the rim, shatter the backboard type of dunks. The types of dunk that will make you get out of dodge on the next one. He dunked the ball so hard one time that when it went through the net, it bounced off the ground so hard it hit my teammate in the face, breaking his nose. It was a psychological fear he had over his defenders and I loved it!

We lost that game pretty bad. I think we lost by as many rebounds Omarion had that night which needless to say, was a lot. After the game I saw him talking to some guy who turned out to be the coach of his prep school team.

He introduced himself, "King motherfucking Brady! How you doing, baby boy? My name is James Lewis and I'm the coach here at North Carolina for North Carolina Prep. We play the best competition throughout the year and all of our players go to Division I Colleges. Most of these colleges send the players here to prepare them for things such as the SAT/ACT and the college level type of environment and sport's schedule. They rank the top 25 prep and post graduate programs and right now, we are currently ranked number two. After watching you play this weekend, I think adding you to our roster would definitely put us over the top. You played against three of my players this weekend, including Omarion. We play at a pace that I think fits your game just fine. I'm going to be talking to your coach. We definitely want you! This is not just any school, King. It costs $5,000 per semester and $10,000 a year. That's a college tuition, but it's a college environment. What do you think?"

"I think it's a great opportunity and I accept. I just have to talk to my AAU coach about it, who is also my guardian. He's been talking to me about it the past two days so it shouldn't be a problem."

Two weeks later, I was headed to prep school.

When I first left for prep school, I didn't know what to expect. I was a little nervous but I knew it couldn't be worse than prison. I was excited and anxious to see how it was going to be. I mean, outside of actually playing basketball, I imagined a military type of school with a crazy daily boot camp regimen. I definitely didn't want to go from one extreme to another, but this was my second chance and I wanted to make the most of it. My new coach picked me up from the airport and as we drove to the school, all I could think was, I'm a long ass way from home! I don't know if he took the scenic route, but all I could see was country, dirt roads, and trees. We were clearly in the boonies. Right in the middle of bumble fucking nowhere. I was starving so we stopped at a place called Bojangles. I never in my life heard of a place called Bojangles but that shit sounded like a place on a farm. When we finally got to our destination, there was a house full of the players from the team. The big fella, as I called him, greeted us at the door.

We all introduced ourselves. There were 12 of us and six rooms so there were two players per room. I didn't recognize anyone outside of the big fella, so I decided to room with him.

Coach Lewis held a team/house meeting to let us know what to expect for the upcoming year.

"Fellas, fellas, fellas. Look around at your new teammates. These are your brothers. This is your new home. This is your new family. You all were handpicked by me and my assistants to come together for something special. When I say special, I mean we put this team together for one specific reason: to be the best damn high school team ever! No team has ever been assembled with all 12 players being ranked in the top 50 players in the country. This is causing a media frenzy in the sports world so much that ESPN wants to do a documentary on us. As the year goes on, you all will be under a microscope. There will be cameras everywhere and at all times so I expect you to conduct yourselves in a manner that is suitable. It's my job to not only see that you all graduate, but that you also get a full scholarship to the college of your choice.

There's an in house chef who comes and cooks twice a day so you won't ever be hungry. We also have 10 tutors who travel with us so you don't fall short on your grades. I did say travel with us because we have a schedule of at least 50 games this season. With a schedule like that, y'all have to be mentally strong as well as in the best shape of your life. That's why starting at 5am tomorrow, we will be at Duke Football stadium working on conditioning."

All of our jaws dropped.

"Nigga!" I worded to the big fella. "Wallace Wade!?"

"That's right," Coach continued. "Wallace Wade steps. We're going to run tomorrow and condition before you go to school. So I expect you all to get a nice full rest and be ready at 5am sharp. You're early if you're there early. You're late if you're there on time! I will leave your ass and it's a lot tougher to run those stadium steps alone!"

Coach Lewis had a very militant tone to his voice so we knew he meant exactly what he said. I didn't want to make a bad impression so I knew I was going to sleep early. Getting up at 5am to me wasn't a big deal because that was close to the same wake up time in prison.

Rooming with the big fella seemed decent. We didn't talk much that first night. I guess we were both scared and anxious of the workout we had the next day. I went to sleep but kept waking up every 30 minutes thinking I was late to the bus. I actually fell asleep and had a dream I missed the fucking bus. When I woke up, it was only 3:45am. After that, I decided to just stay up the rest of the time. Around 4am, the big fella woke up and used the phone. It was the same as when I saw him in the hotel lobby at the tournament. He didn't know I was awake as I sat there and listened to him pray with his mother on the phone. With her being in prison and them praying over the phone, it put things into perspective for me. In that moment, I realized how my family lives vicariously through me. I felt a sense of responsibility. Chill bumps came over me as I thought to myself, you were chosen for a reason. I knew that the only thing standing in the way of my dreams was time. I jumped right out of the bed with a new attitude and positive energy. I had a tough day ahead of me but when I thought about some of my friends and family who had never even been 15 minutes outside of where they came from, I put myself in a grateful and humbling state of mind. Prison was hard; Basketball was easy!

On the way to the stadium, a couple players were still half asleep on the bus and a couple were just real quiet. Me? I was all the way hype and fully awake. I had on my headphones and I was singing whatever was playing at the time. Even the coaching staff was quiet. I didn't like when it was all quiet and everyone was all serious. I know there's a time and place for everything, but I also wanted everyone to be comfortable. Confident. Hype. Just like I was. As we pulled up to Duke University's campus, I was in awe. I always wanted to go to college but this was my first time ever on a college campus. I thought about all the possibilities as we walked toward the football stadium. I felt limitless.

"Fellas," Coach Lewis started. "Welcome to Wallace Wade Stadium. There are 56 rows of over 200 steps here. Your job is to walk down to the very bottom and sprint to the very top. Me and my assistants are spread out so you can't cheat. I'll be on the other side with my binoculars to see if anyone cheats. If I catch you cheating, no matter who it is, you're going home and you will be suspended indefinitely from my program. Bottom line, DON'T FUCKING CHEAT! If you'll cheat on me, you'll steal from me. And I fucking hate thieves. If this shit was too much or wasn't possible, I wouldn't have your ass doing this. This is not a punishment; it's conditioning. Just another obstacle standing in the way of your dreams. You got one hour. This is a team. If everyone doesn't make it within that hour, we'll be back this afternoon after school, in the hot ass sun. You decide. You're only as strong as your weakest link. Now GO!"

We all took off at a great pace. The first three rows were fairly easy. The next three were more difficult. The three rows after that even more difficult. I was just trying to keep pace with the rest of my team. I wasn't in the back or anything and I was keeping a great pace, but I could slowly feel my body tightening up on me. By the time we got to the 25th row, I was dead! I mean literally throwing up, legs shaking, full-blown headache, my mouth was dry as hell, and I felt dehydrated. I stopped to take a look back and get some rest. As I looked around the stadium, we were all spread out. I was somewhere in the middle but I didn't feel bad because all the other players were taking rest breaks too. While I was halfway finished on the 25th row, there were a couple players who were so far behind that I knew they weren't going to make it in that one hour. That shit just pissed me off.

I heard Coach Lewis on the bullhorn, "30 fuckin minutes! Get y'all asses up and run!

Next time I see any of y'all sitting down, we are going to come back regardless of who makes it!"

I put my headphones on and took off. It was a lot easier to run with my headphones on because I wasn't thinking about what I was actually doing at the time. It was a full distraction for my mind. I eventually finished in 45 minutes. I finished second, coming in behind the big fella who finished in 40 minutes. As we sat there, I knew we still had 15 minutes to spare before the hour was up. There were a couple of guys falling way behind so I told the big fella I was going back.

"What!?" He yelled.

"Aye, I'm going back. You can stay! But if we're only as good as our weakest link, then imma try and push them to the finish line."

So I went back to row 43 and ran the rest of the way with my teammates who were last. We barely made it. We were actually 30 seconds late. Coach Lewis sat there with this puzzled look on his face.

"Alright. Everybody to the bus. Breakfast is being prepared at the house. I want you to take a shower and get ready for school. Breakfast is at 7am then the bus is taking y'all to school at eight."

After taking showers, we all limped to the kitchen table sore and in pain, but fully dressed in school uniform and prompt for breakfast. Man it was a feast! Pancakes, sausage, eggs, omelets, bacon, biscuits, french toast, grits, etc. If it was a breakfast food, it was there! I was in heaven. That breakfast made me forget about how Coach was trying to kill us an hour ago in conditioning. We all sat there and ate as a team, Coach included. I didn't want to be the one to address the elephant in the room, but since another player and I were late with conditioning, I had to ask coach.

"So Coach, what's the play for tonight's practice?"

He turned to me with an evil grin on his face and slowly took a sip of his orange juice. "Well, to be honest with you, nobody ever made Wallace Wade stadium steps in an hour! I did that to push you guys and see how naturally tough you were. I saw you finished second and still got back up and helped out your teammate. In the past, we pushed teams before you to make the time in 1 hour and 15 minutes. You all made it in only one. You're special. Uniquely different from all other teams in the past because we specifically recruited the best of the best at each position. Now I have to push you guys even harder. Don't ever get content or stagnant! I'll see you tonight for practice!"

The uniform we had to wear to school was khakis and a light blue shirt with a tie. I was reluctant to put it on but when I got dressed and looked around at my teammates, we all looked very professional. Like a bunch of teenage businessmen. This was a lot better than sitting in a prison jumpsuit anyway so I had no complaints. I didn't hesitate to share those experiences with my teammates who didn't want to wear the uniform.

We were 12 kids from literally all over the world with one common goal. To obtain our goal, we all had to come together for the better of the team. Living together brought us a lot closer much faster than any other team with whom I had ever been associated. There were fights, arguments, and disagreements daily, which in turn made us a better team. We were strong and there for each other. We all were home sick but basketball made us a family. When one person was down and didn't have energy, it was another's job to lift him up and carry us as a team. We laughed together, cried together, ate together, and lived in the same house. Whenever one person went out, we all went out. The whole city knew us basically because it was a basketball city. And we were right in the middle of everything. I was one of the shortest people on my team and I'm 6'4". So you can imagine how hard it was to walk through a mall with 12 players who all are 6'4" and taller. We had three guys who were 7 feet. That alone drew a lot of attention.

After a while, I got used to things. It took about a month, but things became routine. The soreness from the tough practices started to feel good! We could physically see our bodies changing; We all were running faster, getting stronger, and were mentally tougher than ever before and we were running Wallace Wade stadium steps in less than 45 minutes. Practice started getting boring because we always went against ourselves, so we were looking forward to our first game against some great competition. Coach Lewis could see the intensity of practice going down so he decided to set up a scrimmage against a local Division II College. The game was against an HBCU and was open to the public and students. The energy and the turnout was crazy! They had the band playing, dancers twerking just as hard as the regular students in the crowd, and music blaring as we warmed up. I don't know what it is about basketball players and bad ass women, but we were in paradise. Flexing extra hard just because of the energy in the room. I loved it.

Our warm up line definitely set the tone for how the game would go. Windmills, 360's, through the legs, and these were just the dunks I was doing. I was just as athletic as everybody else on my team even though I was one of the shortest. We put on a highlight fest of dunks. It was so bad that the crowd literally stood up and was on the court facing our side to watch us. US! Imagine that feeling. Fresh out of prison and now you're in this environment! All I could think to myself was I'm about to kill these niggas! Coach Lewis ended up not starting me because he wanted to play with the lineup. It offended me at first, but then I just sat back and thought how I was going to dominate the game. The big fella was dominant from the jump ball, scoring our first 16 points single handedly. He either was dunking the ball or getting offensive rebounds off of our missed shots and putting it back in. They called a quick timeout and coach immediately changed the lineup and subbed players.

"We're not letting up. This is a statement game! If I see anybody not giving 100 percent, your ass is gonna be sitting by me!"

I kind of laughed to myself but I understood that coach was trying to push us to perfection. We scored on our first eight possessions with either a dunk or an easy lay-up so I already knew how they were going to adjust coming out of timeout. I was expecting them to play a zone defense since we were unmatched inside and I knew ball movement would be key. I didn't want them to have time to set up their zone defense, so I wanted us to score quick and easy baskets in transition and through our own defense. So I picked my man up 94 feet. I was in the best shape of my life and I wasn't playing long so I could go all out on defense. It was like a chess match. Turn him, turn him, turn him, and then apply a little pressure without reaching. I let my match up come down the court two times without reaching or going for the steal. I knew I had him because I turned him five times before he even got to half court. The third time down, I turned him twice and then went all out for the steal.

After my first steal, he was fairly close so I just did a quick layup. They immediately took the ball out. This time, I turned him three times before I went all out for the steal. Once I stole it,

I knew he was surprised so he didn't run back on defense, It allowed me to have a little show time so instead of just doing a regular dunk, I did the same dunk that I used to do growing up with my brothers. I bounced the ball off the ground hard enough for it to bounce up in the air as a pass to myself. Then I jumped as high as I could, catching it in the air and dunking it backwards. The crowd was on fire. People didn't do shit like this in regular basketball games. This was something people only did in dunk contests so you can imagine the electricity in the building. It got so loud in there that you couldn't hear a single damn thing. After I dunked the ball, I acted like I was going to let up and go back down court. I knew they would throw the ball to my man around half court because he was their only ball handler. So I anticipated the pass perfectly. My back was turned toward him but I quickly turned around as they passed it his way. Another quick steal not even 15 seconds after the last. I took off with the ball in transition and he took off with me. I knew he had to be embarrassed because this was my third straight steal on him.

He chased me down in an all-out effort to steal or stop me from scoring. As I looked back, I just so happened to see one of my teammate's jerseys following us on the play. He was running just as hard. So I dropped the ball back with an around the back pass but I continued forward as if I were laying the ball up. By the time the defender figured out that I had passed the ball behind me, my teammate was already up in the air about to dunk the ball. I mean as soon as

I turned around, the defender literally had my teammate's nuts on his forehead. He almost cleared him by jumping straight over him. As he fell and my teammate dunked the ball, you could see the embarrassment on his face. He looked like he wanted to cry. That face and moment of defeat was exactly what Coach Lewis wanted from us. Coach already knew we had exceptional talent. But he also knew that if we weren't pushed, that talent would stay stagnant and not exceed.

In that moment, in the midst of all the chaos and noise from the students, band members, cheerleaders, etc. running on the court, I realized what Coach Lewis had been preaching since our first day at Wallace Wade. I looked over at him and he wasn't excited or anything. He was calm and reserved. He looked over at me with a still face with absolutely no emotion. And he just nodded his head at me and worded 'next play' with his lips. As excited as I wanted to be, I knew exactly what he meant. We ended up winning that game by nearly 50 points. That was the game that changed our lives! Well at least socially. Everybody in the city heard about how bad we beat a college team and we were the talk of the town. It was funny because we were in high school and were being compared to college teams like Duke, UNC, Wake Forest, and NC State. Those colleges were familiar with our prep program because there were several of our former players who ended up attending these universities.

Our home gym was in the process of being built so we practiced at either Duke University or UNC. After we would practice and the other teams would come in, we could feel the tension in the room. I knew it was just jealousy. The big fella was predicted to be the number one pick in the NBA draft for the next couple of years. He didn't have to go to college. And the way he played and just dominated games, I didn't think he even needed college! Another reason they were mad or felt some type of way was because they knew that their schools were recruiting pretty much all of us to come there next season. It wasn't just their school though. It was pretty much every college in North Carolina and the rest of the country that was recruiting us. Since we were getting so much media attention from ESPN, we had a target on our back. I knew teams were going to be coming for us since we were the team to beat but I embraced it.

The season started and we went on a 10 game winning streak. Our average margin of victory was 20 points. This made us more confident but also made other teams and players that weren't a part of our program more envious. We were the talk of basketball, period. The annual Christmas tournament was a week away starring a couple of the top prep programs in the country. Five of the top 20 schools were playing in the tournament including our school's rival, Oak Hill Academy. They were the defending champs, ranked number one and we were number two. We both pretty much dominated the other teams and it was time for us to meet up for the championship game. They televised the game live on ESPN and we played at North Carolina State's main gym. That game was so packed and a sold out show. Even the college players who were hating and jealous of our team were in attendance. Cameras, lights flashing, reporters, news anchors, etc. This was the game to watch. It was an environment like none other I had ever experienced. I was nervous as fuck! It wasn't the people or the environment I was nervous about.

It was living up to my own expectations. In a game of this magnitude, I knew all eyes were on the big fella, including attention from the other team. This was the perfect opportunity to show the world that we were a lot more than just a one man show.

As soon as the game started, they went into a zone defense. They also went into a box and one against the big fella. Basically, they had two players shading him at all times which left three defenders to try to stop the other four of us. We were scoring so easily that they had to switch their defense. At the end of the first half, we were winning 62 to 45. Oak Hill made the proper adjustments and surprised us with a full court press defense. Catching us off guard, they went on a 10 and 0 run. We only had a six point lead and the momentum seemed to be in their favor. When I finally subbed back in the game, I knew that we had to swing the momentum from them back to us. By that time, the whole crowd was against us. The funny thing was, I liked it better that way.

I huddled my team up while Oak Hill shot free throws.

"Aye! Look around! Look in the stands. They all against us. Now look in this circle and in that bench. It's us versus them. Even the refs are fuckin' cheating. We the best team but that makes us the underdog because whenever we step on the floor, it's us versus the opponent, the refs, and the crowd. Every fuckin body! Big fella. You the best player in the country. Period. It don't matter if you can't get it going offensively, dominate the game in defense! That goes for all of us. It ain't no such thing as a bad day in defense. We can score whenever we want. We just need to get some stops. Let's tighten the fuck up and play TEAM defense. You help me, I help you!"

Then we took the ball out and started playing team basketball. I mean making all the correct passes, playing great team defense, and slowly but surely stealing the momentum back from the crowd. There were five minutes to go in the game and we had the lead by eight points. We knew that they were going to make their final push, so I wanted to put our foot on their necks. We had to make a statement and I don't think we did that up to that last five minute mark. I took it upon myself to lead the charge I scored on my defender with ease two or three times in a row. They immediately went into a zone defense again just like I thought. So instead of trying to score on my defender again, I called the big fella for some pick and roll action. I knew the paint was going to be clogged up because he demanded so much attention from the defense so I drove and passed it out for a wide open 3 pointer. Then I did the same thing the very next play. We went from being up 8 points to being up 16 all within two minutes. They called their last timeout so I knew that things would get a lot more intense the last three minutes of the game. The crowd was almost quiet as we walked back on the court. I don't know if they were mad that we were winning or just in disbelief. Oak Hill ran two players at me as soon as we secured the defensive rebound to try and get the ball out of my hands.

I didn't mind at all.

It was time for the big fella to bring us home. He already had 15 rebounds and 6 blocks. Coach Lewis told us to throw him the ball down court every time for the rest of the game and the big fella delivered. He scored as soon as we threw him the ball. He did a quick spin move and a nasty two handed dunk that looked like the damn goal broke. I mean if you had any doubts about why he was projected to be the number one pick, any speculation was gone after this one play.

The crowd was going crazy. As he went to the free throw line, I just watched the crowd's reaction to his dominance. I just thought to myself, this kid is special. I knew his story and I could actually feel his pain. He vented through basketball just like I did.

See, basketball was more than just a game. A win for us was a win at life where we had taken so many losses. It was a sense of hope. A voice that just needed to be heard.

We went on to win the game by 25 points and in a convincing fashion. We sent a message to the sports world and it felt good. It was the first time I had ever seen Coach Lewis smile so I knew we did something big! We were now ranked the number one high school team in the country and were being documented by ESPN every step of the way. Cameras followed us from our grueling morning Wallace Wade conditioning to our extensive NBA career-like traveling schedule. They were on the buses and even in the dining room when we ate at the house. It became natural and routine, yet again. We became used to the cameras and attention and we were local heroes. Our school's basketball program was sponsored by Nike and after we beat Oak Hill, they flooded us with all the athletic gear you could possibly want. We got shoes three months before they were released to the public, the coolest book bags, socks, travel bags, and sweat suits. I mean so much stuff that I used to send my brothers and friends stuff back home in

Atlanta. Whenever we went out, we would go out as a team. When we went to the mall, we would spend more time taking pictures and signing autographs than actually going to the mall to shop. The cool thing about it was that nobody acted different. We were all just kids chasing a dream as the cameras and extra attention wasn't a distraction for us. We were a real family, living together with one goal in mind and our team chemistry was nearly perfect. No one was envious of the next. Besides, we were all being recruited by major schools so we just genuinely enjoyed each other's company and uplifted one another.

Coach Lewis kept all the outside hoopla on campus away from us. He said it was all a distraction. Half of the time we found things out from our classmates and other people outside of the team.

We went on a 20 game winning streak, breaking the school's previous record by 10 games. We had no signs of slowing down. All we wanted was a national championship and anything less than that was an unsuccessful season. One day at practice, we were playing around talking trash while a scout from Duke was there. He decided to chime in and this sparked an interesting conversation about if we could beat Duke or not. Of course we felt like we could beat them! We felt like we could beat anybody outside of a team with Michael Jordan on it. I mean, we had to think this way. Aaron, the scout from Duke didn't even think we could compete. He expressed this to Coach Lewis and gave him his reasons. True Coach Lewis style, one week later, we had an unofficial scrimmage against them.

It was surreal until the jump ball. I didn't know what we had gotten ourselves into until I was blindsided by a screen from a guy who was 6'9" and 260 lbs. I hit the floor so hard that I bit my tongue. All that ran through my mind was, shit... this is going to be a long game! They were the most fundamentally sound and solid team I had ever played. It seemed like they were all at least two times stronger than us. It felt like we were playing against the fucking monsters from Space Jam! They knew how to hit you legally within the confines of the game and still be mind strong enough to not get into a physical altercation with you. I mean, they would elbow us, grab us, throw us on the ground, and not say a word. I don't even think they had facial expressions.

They may have been robots or at least that's how it felt. They were clearly the better team. I mean they literally beat our asses.

Duke beat us in every statistical category you could name. The best offensive playbook ever known to man. They almost scored during every offensive possession. Not only were we embarrassed but we were mentally beat up as well. The fashion in which they beat us was very demoralizing but also in its own way, very humbling. I think nobody had a good game for us outside of the big fella.

After the game, nobody said a word. We shook hands and walked to the bus. You could hear a pen drop on a bus that was usually filled with laughs, jokes, pranks, and hype men. We rode in 20 minutes of dead silence as we pulled up to our house.

Coach Lewis got up out of his seat first and slowly turned to face us all.

"Anybody can be beat. Humble pie is the best pie, but revenge is a dish best served cold!" Then he walked off the bus in a dramatic fashion. Nobody moved for about five minutes.

I guess we were trying to figure out what the hell Coach was talking about. We went in the house and ate dinner where it was just as silent. Early the next morning, I could hear the big fella moving around the room. Initially I thought he was going to talk to his mother like always, but this time he was getting dressed. I asked him where he was going.

"Wallace Wade," he said.

"Wait. Wallace Wade? Hold up, all of us or just you?" "Just me. The bus will be here in 10 minutes."

Then he went downstairs. As he walked to the bus, I was right behind him. I threw on some sweats and woke up my teammates. He didn't even know we were about to roll out with him. He looked at me in shock.

I shrugged. "We only as strong as our weakest link, right?"

Big fella just smiled and put his headphones back on. Coach Lewis had no idea we went to Wallace Wade without him. When he saw us coming through the doors on our way back from the stadium, he just smiled as he watched us walk by, drenched in sweat. He knew we had work to do but he also saw that we were willing to put in that work. That scrimmage didn't even count but it showed us how much work we had to put in for years to come.

When practice rolled around, all the fun and games were over. It was back to the basics.

We focused primarily on strength and conditioning and executing plays. You would have thought we lost a game in the real season the way we were practicing. A week went by and we were getting tired of beating up on each other in practice so we focused our attention on getting ready for our next opponent.

Our next game wasn't for another two weeks because we had finals in school. We had two tutors and everything seemed to be going fine until we learned that three of our players were in jeopardy of failing classes. So like the family Coach Lewis told us we were, and with all the extra time on our hands from not having practice, we all tutored each other. There was additional help provided by our tutors who traveled with us. We all knew the importance of us staying together. It was a team thing. A team concept. It was kind of like a puzzle. Each of us had a piece to contribute. No matter how big or how small, if you took a piece away, it wasn't going to work. Two weeks passed and it was time to take the finals. Some of us had the same classes so we didn't get to see our other teammates until later that day. We only had time for brief conversations and handshakes in between classes.

I was anxious to get the day over so we could finally get back in the gym. Our new gym wasn't open yet, but Coach Lewis already had the keys. We had a nice long and hard welcome back practice that afternoon with only two days to get prepared for our next game. Grades didn't post until the following week so we were guaranteed to play at least one more game together.

Last time we laced up, we got our asses kicked by Duke. Nobody forgot that feeling and I made sure of it in practice. Even though that game didn't count on any of our records, the same exact feeling lingered. I kind of felt sorry for the next team because I knew the way we were going to bounce back was going to be merciless. No prisoners. We needed it for our morale and there was a chance that was going to be our last game together.

We traveled to Washington DC after our second practice. We wore all black instead of our regular travel uniforms so we could make a statement. Since we didn't know if this was actually our last game together, Coach Lewis decided to do something special for us. As we were getting dressed for the game, Coach came in with a duffel bag full of our new uniforms. They were all black with gold stitching and numbering. The jerseys also had our names on the back and were gold with maroon stitching. They were so dope and much different from our last ones. He told us to remember the moments of now and shook each and every last one of our hands firmly, thanking us individually. That shit brought a tear to my eye. It didn't dawn on me that there was a possibility of us splitting up and not finishing what we started. I really was in denial. I couldn't even imagine what the house would be like without those guys, let alone what the team would be like. We lived and did everything together so we were all like brothers. We knew each other's family from phone calls, visits, and stories. We covered for each other from having to be alibis for girlfriends to covering our asses with Coach Lewis. They made it easy whenever I was home sick. Losing somebody was going to be like losing a family member. Everyone could tell we started to get a little emotional so they brought us another surprise. The coaching staff came into the locker room with shoe boxes and each shoe box had our name and number on it.

When I opened my box my mouth dropped. "Oh shit!"

Nike sent us some all black and gold Flightposites that weren't coming out till the spring.

It was like they were made for us because they went perfectly with our jerseys. They were all black with some crazy cool design on them and had our number stitched on the back in burgundy. They were the dopest shoes I had ever seen in my life. Along with the shoes were black and burgundy Nike socks with the gold trimming to match. I was too hype!

"Damn, y'all!" I yelled out. "I knew Nike was my favorite shoe, but they just solidified their spot in the Hall of Fame in my closet! I don't even want to play in these, Coach. They too clean!"

Everybody started laughing and it was just a priceless moment. I looked around the room and everyone was smiling. If this was our last game together, this was how it was supposed to be. As we walked out of the locker room to warm up for the game, the crowd's reaction to our jerseys and shoes was crazy. I didn't even want to play in my shoes because I didn't want to scuff them. I wasn't the only one though. My whole team was looking down at their shoes checking for scuffs and wrinkles.

Coach started a new line up that night but it didn't bother me. I was anxious to see how we executed and I was too busy flirting with the girls in the crowd. DC had all the bad ladies! A couple of my teammates were from the DMV area so they used to tell us stories, but it wasn't anything like actually being there. The intensity of the crowd was matched by our new uniforms. We were ready!

About five minutes into the game, we were executing well but only up by 6 points. The other team was feeding off the crowd's intensity. Most teams played us closely in the beginning, but eventually we pulled away with the lead. I always thought it was better getting a team's best shot against you rather than their worst because I feel like it's better to beat an opponent at their best over their worst. Then mentally they know, they can't fuck with you.

When coach put me in the game, the intensity had calmed down. It was the perfect timing! I still had all my energy from when the game first started so it was easy to attack their weaknesses that I saw from the bench. My instant offense and energy led us to a 15 point lead going into halftime. When the second half started, Coach decided to switch the lineup. He still didn't start me, but we didn't miss a beat. We laughed and joked on the bench as we watched what could possibly be our last game together. After the game, we were like rock stars, signing autographs and taking pictures. A bitter sweet feeling for sure, but just a reminder to not take moments for granted.

That was the longest bus ride back home it was completely silent the entire ride. You would have thought we lost the damn game. I wanted to crack a joke or something to bring us up but everyone's mood was so down. Time went on and we had to learn how to play without the big fella. Since he was our number one option and all of our offense pretty much ran through him, we had to play a lot faster we instantly became a guard oriented team, pressing teams in a 2-1-2 full court press. That gave me an advantage because I could play multiple positions in this defense. Ironically, all of our numbers went up after we lost the big fella. Mine went up the most, averaging 18 points, 7 assists, 7 rebounds, and 5 steals over the next month. We went on an eight game winning streak, building the anticipation to play against the number two ranked school in the country.

Practices got more intense when we learned that we would be playing on ESPN that game. Not only playing on TV, but the game was also moved to the college campus where we were practicing. Moments like those are what we lived for! It was the perfect audience and platform to showcase ourselves as players and our abilities to work well with our team. It was basically like an organized All Star Game. I mean, everyone wasn't just good, they were exceptional players! There were 10 players with scholarship offers on each team with a few who had already given verbal commitments. This game was the best versus the best but I remained focused. As the game was starting, a few of my teammates seemed a little nervous from missing a couple of easy layups to missing some wide open shots. I didn't know what had gotten into them. Maybe it was the 10,000 people screaming from the stands who actually came to see a high school game. Or maybe it was because it was being televised on ESPN and viewable by millions. I'm not sure. But whatever the reason, we weren't playing like ourselves.

A quick 12 point deficit took us into a timeout. I didn't panic because I knew we were just missing shots, so I took it upon myself to lead the charge. Since we were missing shots and not getting rebounds, it was tough to set up our press defense. I called the next three plays for me to be put in an isolation situation. Then scored all three times. The basket started looking bigger and I was feeling good. Two deflected passes let to steals and assists to me scoring easy layups. I was on a roll. The team fed off my energy. We went from being down 12 points to being up 4 points. They started to double team me, and that's when the game really changed. They must have shot at least 90 percent from the field in the 3rd quarter. They weren't missing a single shot. Before we knew it, we were down 20 points going into the 4th quarter. Naturally, we had our heads hung real low. We were getting blown out and embarrassed in front of the whole world. If they were the better team, I could live with that. But giving up and just no longer competing… I just didn't have that in me.

During the timeout, I was very vocal.

"Y'all playing like some bitches! Like y'all scary as hell and nervous!"

I was frustrated because I was getting double-teamed and couldn't get my teammates to score. So once again, I took it upon myself to make a way. I came out in the 4th quarter firing away. I figured if I pushed the ball in transition, then they couldn't double-team me at all. It worked. It actually worked. I forced the issue using my speed and it just put pressure all on the other team. My efforts weren't enough to come back and we did end up losing the game by 8 points.

I finished with 33 points, 14 rebounds, 6 steals, 5 assists, and 3 blocks. I was a real stat stuffer. My life changed right after the 4th quarter of that game because before we got back to our house, I literally had 15 college offers. We all knew it was going to be different playing without the big fella, but no one expected me to merge into the number one option on the team.

The season went on and the dream of me going to college was even closer. My teammates and I all decided to take the SAT's together. When we got our scores back, the whole team qualified and we were all eligible to play NCAA basketball. The SAT's didn't make me nervous at all. I ended up getting a 1350, which was the second highest score on my team. My score upset me though because I didn't know that you were only being graded by the questions you answered and not the questions you didn't. I literally tried to answer every question given to me. Just knowing that I qualified for the NCAA was good enough for me, but my score opened up the floodgates for college offers. Narrowing down the school options was easy for me, I just held on to the schools with the best business programs and basketball teams to match. After taking my official five college visits, my decision was very clear to me where I wanted to play. You see, every school offered me money to sign. Some a little more than others, there was one school, however, who offered me no money. That is what stood out to me because they spoke less about sports and more about what my future interests were aside from basketball. Prior to my visits, I did research on each university so I was already familiar with their business program. Signing day came, and I chose Alabama Technical Institute.

V

Going to college meant the world to me. I was first handedly seeing my dream come into fruition. The last year and a half of my life happened so fast. I went from one extreme to another and I wasn't going to take it for granted. Being the first person in my family to go to college was definitely something that made us all proud; I reminded myself of this every time I got home sick.

I chose the Alabama Tech for a few reasons. The first reason was because we were bringing in a top five recruiting class, so I knew the team was going to be good. The second reason was because we were the second college with 10 nationally televised games against ranked opponents. That was a huge deal... and Duke was first! Thirdly, they went all the way to the sweet 16 the year before during the March Madness tournament and they were bringing back three starters. Another really important reason was that the university was only three hours away from home so my family could come watch my team play. I was considered a high profile player due to my recruiting status coming out of high school. That meant I was under the microscope.

Coach G explained that to us in our first team meeting during opening week.

"Gentlemen, welcome to the Alabama Tech's basketball program. You are now a part of a program with a winning tradition, an accelerated academic program, and you also inherited a bullseye on your back. There are no professional teams in the state of Alabama so you guys are held to that standard. Accept it. Embrace it. The sooner, the better. I know this is college and this is a time for you to have the time of your life, but you are not held to the same standard as your peers. You are a reflection of the program and anything you do in the public eye will be seen as such. Some of you guys have already been here, so I'm counting on you to explain it to the new ones."

Coach wasn't lying either. Things were different there. Everybody already knew you and identified with you. From all of the billboards around the city, to being all in the newspapers and magazines. The attention we got around campus and in the city was a bit overwhelming.

Sometimes it was cool going to parties and being the center of attention when it came to girls, but other times, we had days of frustration like everybody else and didn't feel like signing autographs or taking pictures.

School was challenging but captivating at the same time. Business was my major because it just made sense for my mindset. I didn't want to work for anyone so I wanted to learn how to run my own business. Most of my classes were stadium classes with over 100 students. With every class I attended, I wanted to make sure I sat on the first row. Classes were mostly lectures and note taking but I wanted my professors to see my face that way they could see how serious I was about college.

Growing up, there were all these stereotypes about the male athlete being all brawn and no brain. Especially a black man. As I looked around my Mass Communications class and stared at the students, I caught myself in deep thought. There were probably around 150 students total, and only 25 were black. Out of that 25, fifteen of them were a part of the athletic program, whether it was basketball, football, track or whatever. The rest of the class was Asian, Indian, and mostly white. That landscape put me in a perspective of recognizing what was at hand. It wasn't just students I was looking at, it was a representation of the world. And I was a representation of my family. We all came from different facets of life and it didn't matter how we got there, we were there.

It was the starting line. Probably not a fair shot trying to manage practice, games, school, and travel, but my school was almost $18,000 per semester and I was on a full scholarship. So a little extracurricular activity was an even trade.

Things started becoming routine like most big changes in my life. Practice hadn't started yet, so we were just doing individual practices and conditioning. My schedule was very time consuming. As an athlete, I didn't have too much time to myself. I guess that was also part of that trade. My whole day was pretty much planned out starting with 6:30 a.m. conditioning. I guess those Wallace Wade morning runs came in handy because I was used to getting up early. My days didn't end until about 9 p.m. and I would be so tired that I would just go to sleep. Whenever I talked to family and friends from back home, they had all these crazy questions for me about school. My aunt would talk to me about simple things like school, staying out of trouble, and wanting to send me care packages. My brothers would ask me about the team, how I was playing, and when I was coming home. They were proud of me.

My brothers seeing me go off to college meant more to me than anybody else. It was because we came from the same house and same situation with the same struggle. So having them see me overcome those odds was inspiring and motivating. It still is. It gave them a sense of hope and I wanted to show them that there was more to life than our environment and circumstances. Friends I grew up with were dying, dropping out of school or were locked up. I was right there with them so it was hard not to believe I could have turned out the same way.

Growing up, my aunt told us every day, *it's so easy to get in trouble, and so hard to get out.* I understood that better after I was sitting in a cell for a while.

I had some friends and other classmates from the past that were in other colleges around the country and we stayed in touch through Facebook. A couple of my homeboys from back home played football at Auburn. Auburn was our rival school but it didn't matter because they came to our party and we went to theirs. And even though I was away from home, it was good to always see old friends and classmates at our football games.

We finally started team practices and we were probably a month away before kicking off the season. I was announced as a starter but coach had changed my position. I was 6'4" and 205 pounds. I don't even remember how I got so big. It must have been a combination of going to prison, having a personal chef in prep school, and now this crazy ass UFC style weight trainer that was handling our conditioning and training. I bulked up and coach wanted me to be more of a scorer. Coach G wanted to have two floor generals to run his offense but he also wanted me to carry the load offensively. It wasn't all on me of course as we had a great team. Those guys had made it all the way to the Sweet 16 the previous year. My job was to pick up where they needed help. There was a senior guard starting the year before, so the shooting guard position was wide open. Coach G told me that NBA scouts saw me as a point guard who could score but Coach saw me as a scorer who could pass the ball. The fact that NBA scouts even knew my name was motivation.

A couple weeks passed and we were getting ready for the annual Midnight Madness. The following day was the football team's homecoming so I already knew it was going to be a good ass weekend.

Midnight Madness was basically like a huge pep rally and scrimmage game where we were introduced to the whole university. We also had a dunk and 3 point contest. It was held at midnight and was a way for the students and staff to get a preview of the upcoming season. I definitely left my mark. I lost the dunk contest but I made it to the championship round. I won the 3 point contest by nearly double the amount of the guy who came in second. Then I finished the scrimmage game with a triple double. I had 16 points, 12 rebounds, and 11 assists. Although the game didn't count, the point I was trying to make was clear. I wanted everybody to know that Coach didn't make a mistake when he signed me. I became a fan favorite immediately and was rushed by fans wanting autographs and pictures after the game. It was a humbling experience being praised and recognized for my basketball talents and it was an even better feeling having that platform to talk to all the girls.

I was invited to about 15 different homecoming parties but I decided to throw my own. I spread the word to a couple different groups of females and I also told my teammates. There were parties being thrown by all the fraternities and sororities so I knew people were going to be everywhere. I invited some of my homeboys from back home and some of us met up at the football game earlier that day. People had been tailgating since 8 a.m., drinking and eating good food and just chilling. I wasn't a drinker or a smoker so I was just enjoying the fact that everybody was having a good time. I had never seen or experienced anything like it in my life. There were over 80,000 people around us, most of whom recognized who we were. I figured I made myself a lot more popular after last night's rally, but I wasn't ready for all the extra attention at the football game. Girls were coming up to me hugging me and dudes were giving me handshakes and the older people wanted to take pictures. I just went with the flow. Shit, it was homecoming! It was the best time to be social.

After the game, the festivities continued. Everywhere we went it was jam packed. From gas stations to the Walmart parking lot, it was one of those nights you just knew was going to be memorable. A couple of my teammates and I lived in the same neighborhood as the Q's and the Kappas, two of the biggest fraternities on campus. I just so happened to live right in the middle of each frat house. It was a prime location and easy access to females, so we decided to have the party at my spot. I was approached by both fraternities about joining a little earlier in the semester, so it was easy to politic our way into their party before ours started. Well, ours wasn't like a party. It was more of like a chill, kick back. We wanted to get a couple of bad females to come through and hopefully they liked females as much as we did, you know, G shit. After all, this WAS college and these ladies were going to the parties regardless.

These parties were like some girls gone wild parties so our only plan was to recruit. I invited two of my best friends from high school, Brandon and Corey. They didn't make it to the game but they arrived just in time to go recruit some ladies. I filled them in on the mission and we went to work. The Kappa house was closest, so we went there first. The line was packed outside the door with people trying to get inside.

This shit was better than any of the clubs around. There were females in groups of 8, 5, and 3, and they were all fine. Maybe it was just the atmosphere, but everything was beautiful. I definitely wasn't about to stand in that long ass line so I told my patnas to follow me. As we walked to the front, I felt like a celebrity because over 10 people called my name and came and gave me dap. Then I had a couple ladies I already knew from class come and hug me so that was a good look for whoever was in the line choosing. We got to the front and they let us right in.

The party was jumping. Everybody was drinking and dancing. I think the theme of the party was red cups because that's all you saw. Girls were dancing on girls and with dudes. The sexiest thing in the world outside of sex to me is watching a woman dance. So I was in heaven, but I had to play it cool. After a couple of handshakes and brief introductions, I had a red cup in my hand too. This sexy ass exotic looking girl brought it to me.

"I don't drink, sweetheart!"

She looked at me with that 'I want to fuck you' face. "First time for everything."

Then she just walked off. Her hair was bone straight and parted in the middle and so long, literally to the top of her ass cheeks. She had on all white with no panties and some heels. This chick was bad. She clearly stood out from every other female so far. Once she walked off, she dipped into the crowd so fast that I didn't get a chance to really talk to her. I would have seemed thirsty and desperate if I would have followed her around the room so I just played it cool. Besides, there is always someone watching. This party was full of females. I figured she would come back around. My homies and I were split up, but any time I made eye contact with them, they were definitely at work.

After about an hour and a half, we made our way to the Q party. Their party was just as packed but with a much more rowdy crowd. They were hands down the real partiers, on some Animal House type shit. As soon as we got in, I saw Jacob, our school's starting quarterback. We had two classes and study hall together so we were pretty cool. He was stupid drunk but funny and annoying at the same time. So after a brief conversation, I went on about my business. I made my rounds through the party but this time I was being a little more aggressive, trying to holla at women more here than at the last party. Then I saw the exotic looking chick again. I cut her off to where we had to walk directly in front of each other's path.

She stepped right to me. "Oh hey! How did you like it?" "How did I like what?" I asked her.

"The hunch punch! I made it myself."

Then I laughed. "I told you I don't drink, sweetheart. Besides, you gave me that drink and walked away so fast that I thought you were trying to poison me. I didn't trust it. And what type of name is hunch punch anyway? If I ain't know no better, I'd think you were tryna tell me something."

We both laughed.

"No, silly!" She said. "We call it hunch punch because it's catchy. It does get you pretty fucked up though. So I guess you and your boys are party hopping tonight?"

"Yeah, something like that. More like bringing the party to us. I was trying to talk to you at the Kappa party though. I guess you and your girls are on the same shit we on, party hopping. Unless one of y'all boyfriends is a Q and the other is a Kappa."

"I'm actually here by myself Mr... I'm sorry, what did you say your name was again?"

I paused for a hot second, amused by her actually not knowing who I was. Maybe she does and this is just game, I thought.

"I'm King, sweetheart, and you?"

"King? Is that your government name or nickname, because I'm not going to be calling nobody King and that's not their real name."

"Well maybe you need one in your life." I tried to convince her. She looked at me with an attitude. "One of what?"

"A King! You're a Queen right?"

She smiled as she looked me up and down then before she could say anything, I cut her off.

"Aye, aye, ayyee! You cant't be eye fucking me in public like that. Your boyfriend might get mad!"

"And who said I had a boyfriend?"

"And who said I had a boyfriend?"

"The same person that eye fucked me in public and didn't even tell me her name! And if you don't have a dude, you definitely ain't deny it."

Caught off guard by my witty and timely comebacks and charismatic savvy, she continued the conversation.

"Well Mr. I don't think your name is King, I'm actually here by myself. My twin brother is a Q, and also the starting quarterback for University of Auburn. Our first cousin, who grew up with us after his parents died in a car accident, he's a Kappa. That's why you saw me at both parties. My name is Lorraine. I go to the University of Tennessee. I came down to support my brother and chill for homecoming weekend."

"Damn, those must be some awkward dinners. Who do you go for when we play against Tennessee?"

"My brother of course!"

We laughed and ended up talking for about 30 minutes. I didn't see Brandon and Corey around so I already knew where they were. I wasn't sure if Lorraine was the type to come to our little after party, so I didn't tell her about it at first. Instead, I asked her if she wanted to get some food. We ended up grabbing some Waffle House but it was so packed we just got it to go. I told her that my house was going to be kind of live because my whole plan was to show my homeboys from back home a good time. She was cool with it. I really loved her vibe. Just laid back and went with the flow type of girl. The more I got to know her, the more I wanted her around me.

We went back to my apartment and nobody was there yet.

As we ate our food, Brandon and Corey came in with about five girls. I had lost some of my other teammates from earlier, but they were texting me so I knew they were safe. The vibe of the house was perfect. All the females were getting along and enjoying the night. Nobody was acting siddity or stuck up so I guess the guys did a good job recruiting. I had a four bedroom apartment to myself since no other students had moved in with me yet.

I took Lorraine to my bedroom with me while the others were out drinking and smoking in the other room. Me and Lorraine were vibing perfectly. She kept me wanting more conversation as she gave me a face massage. I never in my life had a face massage so I was feeling amazing. My dick was rock hard from the time we walked in my apartment but I continued to play it cool. I wasn't going to try her unless she gave me a dead on sign. Then we started to kiss. It was real slow and passionate. Those 'I want to make love to you' type of kisses. Of course I had my fair share of lady friends and damn sure wasn't new to this sex thing, but this just felt different. I actually liked her. She was more than just eye candy.

There was just as much substance as it was swag with Lorraine. I figured it was damn near impossible to catch feelings for somebody that soon but she definitely fucked my mind. She mind fucked the shit out of me. I'm sapiosexual, meaning that I'm attracted to intelligence so I knew she was going to be special. I started kissing her shoulders and slowly went down her back. Starting with the top of her neck, I kissed her down her spinal cord slowly. I could tell she didn't want me to stop by the deep and slow moans she made while I was kissing her. Her dress was cut perfectly all the way down her back so I didn't have to move or adjust anything. She was wearing what you would call a real freakum dress.

She tried to take her heels off but I told her to keep them on.

As I got to the top of her ass with my lips, I heard a big ass banging noise at my front door. Whoever it was, was knocking like the damn police, so of course I jumped up to see what was going on. I looked out of my bedroom window and there were about six or seven dudes outside. They saw me look out the window and started banging on it so I told Lorraine to stay in the room while I ran outside. As I was walking out of the room, I heard a big glass shattering noise. These drunken motherfuckers had thrown a big rock through my living room window.

Brandon and Corey ran to the front of the room with me and we walked to the front door. As soon as I opened up the door, some crazy ass football player ran straight in. I didn't waste any time knocking him out. I club punched the hell out of him, a one hitter quitter! He dropped and fell into my glass coffee table and it shattered everywhere. Meanwhile, the friends of this dude I just knocked out were trying to barge in the doors. Next thing I knew, it was an all-out brawl from my living room to the outside front entrance of my apartment. I had no clue what we were fighting over but it didn't matter at that point. I knew I was going to swing on whoever was on the other side of that door. I already knew as soon as that rock went through my window, I was going to act a fool. I picked up a Grey Goose bottle and flat lined one of the guys rushing in. I was really trying to break it on his skull. When his homeboys saw that, they ran out of my apartment. We had to pick up the dude who fell through my coffee table and literally toss him outside. He was bleeding from his hands and arms from the glass on the table. I even thought the other dude was dead because he wasn't moving at all.

Lorraine called the police as soon as everything started so they had been en route for a minute. We left the dude lying there on the ground as we waited for the ambulance to arrive. That's when we discovered that a couple of the girls Brandon and Corey brought back to the house were the girlfriends and sisters of some of the dudes we were fighting. I was so fucking mad so I kicked all those bitches out. I was about to kick Lorraine out too because I thought maybe her brother was next to come over with some drama.

I looked at her. "I'm sorry baby, but I don't think it's safe for you here. I don't know if these niggas comin' back with some bullshit or not. If they do, I don't want you here!"

Lorraine called her cousin to come pick her up. As I walked her to the door, we heard about eight loud ass gunshots. We jumped on the floor and took cover, crawling all over the glass on the floor, pulling Lorraine to the back room. I locked her in my bathroom and walked out. As I got back to the living room, the police had Brandon and Corey sitting up in handcuffs on the couch. Shit happened that fast! The police saw a man lying there on the ground with all the glass on the floor and a broken coffee table and immediately thought we were in the wrong, of course.

I tried to explain what was going on, but the cops didn't want to hear it. They put me in handcuffs and sat me down with my homeboys. They called the ambulance and searched the apartment while we waited for the ambulance to arrive. They found about two ounces of weed and an unregistered, loaded pistol with a beam on it. They also found more liquor in the house along with Lorraine locked in the bathroom. Lorraine tried to explain what happened, but the officers didn't want to hear that either. Nobody admitted to the loaded gun or the weed so they charged me with it since the apartment was in my name.

I didn't think it was serious until I found out all the charges against me: aggravated assault, possession of marijuana, underage drinking, and possession of an unregistered handgun.

All I could think was I was already a convicted felon, so I was real shook. I was spooked but I knew once they heard the story, they would release me.

Instead of trying to hear me out, the cops wanted to be assholes. They held me overnight until Coach came to get me. As we walked out, there were about 20 reporters all in my face. The news spread so fast around the campus. I told Coach G exactly what happened; I knew I could trust him. Besides, I didn't do anything wrong. A simple blood test would show that there was no alcohol or marijuana in my system. The assault charges were going to be easy to get dropped as well because it was as simple as self-defense. I was literally defending myself in my own house. The gun charge was more complicated though. Brandon took ownership of the gun and was going to testify in court to that. Meaning all charges brought against me were going to be dropped. The media had a field day with the event. It was like they wanted me to be guilty.

Every time I cut on the TV or read the school paper, they painted me as some thug ass criminal! Even after a written statement from both sides, including the attorneys, they still made the story look how they wanted it to look.

Of course I was the face of it all because I was the "high-profile" athlete. I could barely walk around campus without being asked a million questions. I knew just how big this situation was when it made its way to Sports Center.

Coach G decided it would be best for me to not practice with the rest of the team since my situation was becoming a distraction. So instead, the coaching staff worked me out individually to stay in shape. Basketball was all I had to turn to when my mind was going crazy. I felt a bid isolated since I couldn't practice with the team, but Coach G kept me in good spirits as we were a week away from our first game. Unfortunately, I couldn't play until after my court hearing. My court date was three days before our first game so I was eager to get it all over with. It wasn't so much court that bothered me; I really just wanted to be able to play in the season opener.

As my court date got closer, the time seemed to go by slower and slower. I kept my focus by concentrating in school and working out. Midterms were going on in school, so it was easy to stay dwelled in my books.

Sitting in court a few days later, I wasn't nervous at all. Everything went as planned and my coach and teammates were all in attendance to show their support. After the two hour session, all charges brought against me were dropped. I was ecstatic! As I walked out, the reporters were trying to get a statement from me but I didn't say a word to them. These reporters, ESPN, the local news, and every other sports show, were the same motherfuckers who were bashing me in the papers and trying to defame my character. I held my head high and didn't look a single reporter in the eye, let alone say a word. I started to feel like I had something to prove and I knew just where to vent my frustrations. Nothing in the world to me was quite like the basketball court. I had a sense of true freedom and liberation every time I stepped on to the court. I left the courthouse and went straight to the gym. I arrived an hour before my teammates or coaches just to shoot around.

After two days of hard practices and trying to catch back up to speed with my teammates, I was ready to play. Game day had finally arrived. It was my first college game and it had been a long time coming! I had been dreaming of this moment for the longest and the moment was finally coming true. I had a rush of déjà vu come over me as I stared at my last name on my jersey and thought to myself, *this is exactly where I'm supposed to be. God doesn't make mistakes!*

Chills came over my body as we made our way to the court; I was all business! I didn't crack a smirk or even glimpse into the crowd because I was so focused. I had complete tunnel vision. It was a sold out game but I couldn't hear anything but the screeches on the floor from our shoes. I remembered this feeling from the past so I knew exactly what kind of game I was going to have. As we warmed up, I made my way to the bench with three minutes to go before tipoff. I had the same routine as always. I looked around the arena and I took it all in before I closed my eyes to pray. While my eyes were closed, mental flashes of the past few weeks consumed my thought process. I got so angry that I started to tear up.

That's when I started praying.

"Father, thank you! Please help me turn this negative into a positive. Amen!"

I kept my prayer short and sweet but direct and to the point. God knew what I was saying.

We were playing against Georgia Tech, another school who also adamantly tried to recruit me. They were in my top five schools until they signed another guard. I wanted them to know they made a mistake so I took them off my list. This game and opponent was just fuel to a flame that was already burning. My tunnel vision consumed me and I didn't shake a single hand as my feet hit the court. As we lined up for the jump ball, one of the Georgia Tech players made a comment towards me.

"I'm surprised they let you out of jail, my nigga! You ain't drop the soap, did you?"

I heard him loud and clear but my silence toward his dumbass comment was even louder.

The ball went up and I purposely stepped down on his foot at the same time. My hands were on my knees so when he looked down, I raised them quick as if I was going for the ball, hitting him right in his face, putting him in a complete daze. The ball got tapped to my teammate and a quick alley-oop to me as I sprinted to the basket. I dunked the ball as hard as I could, watching it spike off the ground and into the crowd. I was super hype but I just kept a straight game face. I sprinted to half court full speed and ran back up toward the baseline like I was doing suicide sprints. I immediately picked my man up, forcing him to pass it and caused a quick turnover. After my teammate stole the ball, he kicked it ahead to me and I touch passed the ball right back to him. He dunked it and yelled to the crowd. I sprinted to half court and right back up to the baseline again. Coach G signaled for a full court press, throwing Georgia Tech off guard. They couldn't get the ball in and got a five second violation. Once we took the ball out, I called for a special.

A special was an out of bounds play for me to get open for a three pointer. I took the ball out, threw it to the wing and set a solid back screen on the defender. At the same time, there was another back side screen for me as I went to the three point line. This play always worked in practice and we ran it to perfection.

If the screen was set right, there would always be three wide open options: the alley-oop play for my big man after my screen, me getting a back screen and an open three pointer, or my other teammate who set the screen for me would be open under the basket as he rolled to the rim.

When I caught the ball on the 3 point line, I already knew I was going to be wide open so I took my time, set my feet, and knocked the 3 pointer down. As soon as the ball left my hands, I ran to the half court line because I knew the ball was going in the net! Georgia Tech finally got the ball in and got down court into a good position. They got a good shot off but ended up blowing a contested layup. As my teammate rebounded the ball, I sprinted the lane. They kicked the ball ahead to me and I unconsciously just pulled up and shot at least a 25 footer in rhythm. I didn't know I was so far back at the time but my momentum and adrenaline carried me through. I held my follow through until I saw the ball go through the net. That shit reminded me of when Sanaa Lathan hit that 3 pointer on Love and Basketball and just kept her hand up on cockiness. Instead of running back up the baseline again, I walked to the bench because they called a timeout. The team was real hype and dapping each other up and signaling to get the crowd hype too. I calmly sat there, real smooth like. This was a nationally televised game on ESPN and the cameras were on me, especially after all the scrutiny the media was throwing at me from the drama that had just ended off the court.

I knew I had to play it cool like I always did. Coach G could see it in my eyes. The anger. The pain. The focus. Coach wasn't the type to put a hold on your game, but rather unleash you. I loved Coach G for that! It was a lot of the reason I chose to come to the Alabama Tech anyway.

Coach huddled us up and kneeled right in front of me.

"Since King got the hot hand, we're going to initiate the offense through him. The next three offensive possessions, we're going to run stack, Bama, and fist!"

Those were all the plays structured for me to get shots or make something happen because it put the ball in my hands. The team was receptive to Coach's call and even told me to be more aggressive. As we came out of the timeout, Coach pulled me aside.

"Go to work!"

I was already in my zone but Coach saying that pushed me even further and made me that much more aggressive. He switched our defense up into a 3-2 matchup zone. We disguised it as

a man defense, catching Georgia Tech off guard once again, forcing a bad shot. I grabbed the rebound and pushed it up the floor. I passed it and got it back, immediately calling fist. Fist was nothing but a pick and roll two man game. I figured they would double-team me coming out of timeout, but I was wrong. They continued to play us man to man and I easily scored all three possessions. I stayed with a straight face the entire game; I was all business!

Going into halftime, I was already well on my way to a triple double. I had 17 points, 7 rebounds, 6 assists, and 2 steals. As I was walking toward the locker room, some media reporters signaled me for an interview. I respectfully declined with a nod as I worded "no thank you" to them.

Standing close by was ESPN. They tried to chime in and ask for a few responses from me as well.

That was when Coach G stepped in.

"King is a special player. For him to come out here and have the type of first half he did says a lot about his character! We all know about the foolishness that went on off the court and he held his innocence the entire time. He handled himself like a respectable young man when there were crazy reports painting him as something he's not and he did it the right way.

He told me before the game that he never wanted to talk to media again and I totally understand why. I mean, can you blame him?"

Then the media started talking to Coach about some other players and the team as a whole. Coach never doubted my innocence for even a split second. If he did, he hid it well. The drama off the court brought us closer on and off the court.

The second half was underway and coach switched the lineup. He moved me to the point because he knew Georgia Tech would switch their defense and would double to try and get the ball out of my hands. He wanted me to initiate the offense and create a bit of a diversion. Coach was right! They came out doubling me damn near when I was taking the ball out. It was a quick 12-2 run and an even faster timeout. The arena was so loud but somehow I could always hear the most random comments. No matter how much I blocked out the crowd, hearing that many people cheering for me gave me a special kind of energy. I could feel the fans rocking! All of this energy mixed with all the pain and preparation to get here, a double team wasn't about to stop my run!

I finished the game with 22 points, 10 rebounds, 10 assists, and 4 steals. Those were PlayStation numbers! The most impressive part was that I only played 25 minutes. I was the talk of town once again but this time for something good. Our highlights were all over Sports Center and we even made the top 10 plays of the week. If I wasn't already a household name, I certainly was after that performance. Talks of the NBA immediately started to surface as my draft stock went up. I was only a freshman and making history. A triple double had never been recorded by a freshman at my school, let alone one with only 25 minutes of playing time. That record and the amount of time piqued the interest of all types of NBA scouts.

After all this hype and positivity, the media attention rubbed some people the wrong way because the following week, I was back under investigation.

When I walked into the locker room for practice, Coach G sat me down to explain what was going on.

"Son," he said, in his drawn out, Alabama accent. "Take a seat! When I recruited you, it wasn't so much of your ability. Don't get me wrong, you have effortless talent but I was most interested in your ambition. Your competitive drive is fueled by your ambition. And from the year that I recruited you up to now, that's something that is unmatched. I don't ever want you to lose that ambition or drive. Promise me you won't. Right now, King! Promise me!"

I sat there kind of baffled on what he was saying.

"Alright Coach. I promise! Damn! But why are you tellin me all this?"

Coach just looked at me, slowly shaking his head. As he tried to speak, he started choking up from the tears.

"Damn Coach, what's up? You alright?" I said with a concerned voice. Then it switched to a nervous and panic ton. "Coach, is it something I did?!"

My stomach started to get butterflies like I already knew what was up. "Coach! What's up? Talk to me!"

Coach looked me right in my eyes. "I'm sorry, son, but the state picked up your case from a couple weeks back. And even though you were cleared of all charges, you being a convicted felon and having an unregistered gun in your apartment is a violation of your probation. So not only does the state want to pick up your case, but the university also has to pull your scholarship."

He was talking really low and crying so I could barely understand him. "I'm sorry Coach. Did you just say I was losing my scholarship?"

Out of everything he just said, that was all I took in. "Are you fucking serious? Coach!

Are you serious?"

He couldn't even look me in my eyes and that's when I flipped out on him.

"How long did you know this Coach? Because I find it hard to believe that all of this could happen over the weekend! Maybe you just wanted me to play in that game to help y'all get a win! I knew I shouldn't have ever come to racist ass Alabama!"

Coach G just sat there in tears shaking his head. He tried to talk but I didn't want to hear that shit so I walked out. I saw a couple of my teammates as I walked through the arena. They tried to speak but I was real short with them. I didn't know if any of them knew the news already, but I didn't even care! I drove to practice that day but I knew if I were to drive at that moment, I probably would have wrecked my car, so I decided to walk home. As soon as I started walking, it started to pour down raining. No lightening. No thunder. Just fucking rain! I was so pissed off that I didn't even care and I just kept walking.

Classmates, students, and other random people who recognized my face stopped and offered me a ride but I didn't even care to stop walking. I just kept going. The thought of actually going back to jail consumed my thoughts. And the fact that I was innocent, again, broke me down and took whatever piece of heart I had left. I looked to the sky with all this anger in my heart and felt like God was doing this on purpose. I was almost sure of it. It was raining hard as hell like it was about to flood or something, but there wasn't a single cloud in the sky. The sun was all the way out and shining brighter than ever. I didn't understand it. It was like the rain was for me!

I finally got home – cold and drenched in rain. I took a hot shower and sat on the floor of the bathtub as the water hit my face. I closed my eyes and just listened to the water. As I sat there, I played different scenarios out in my head. None of which I could actually come to terms with so I thought about this. I wanted to die. I wanted to die so bad, that I asked for it! I literally prayed and asked God to take my life before I did it myself. At the exact moment of me thinking about taking my life, my phone rang. I had never heard that ringtone before because it was an unknown caller calling me. I picked up the phone and tossed it back on the floor of the bathroom. I figured it was some type of reporter or something so I didn't answer. They called me right back. Again, and again, and again. By the sixth ring, I was fucking irritated and ready to curse out whoever was on the other end of my phone!

I answered the phone with an attitude.

"Hello! Why the fuck you keep calling me back to back? This shit better be an emergency!"

Then there was a pause.

"Hello! Can you hear me? Hellooooo!!!"

I couldn't hear anything but breathing on the other end as if somebody was out of breath.

Then a sickly and exhausted voice came on my phone. It was my mother's voice. "King! This is your mother! You sound so angry!"

My mood immediately changed. I hadn't talked to my mother in almost three years. To hear her sound so sick and coughing like that made me focus on her health and not my problems.

"Oh shit. I'm sorry, mom. Where you at? And why do you sound like that? Are you okay?"

She struggled to speak, coughing and pausing until she finally got it all out.

"Son, my doctor said I have less than six months to live. My cancer is in its terminal stage. You didn't recognize the number because I'm in the hospital. Listen carefully because I need you to fill out this paperwork for me. I don't trust your brother with anybody but you. He needs to be around his brother. So I want you to take full custody of him for me in the event that I do indeed only have six months to live. I tried to get in touch with my sister, but you know how she is towards me."

I didn't know what to say. I mean that fast, my whole life was changing. Again. My school problems were minute at that moment, including the possibility of going to jail. Nothing else mattered. All I could focus on was the pain in my mom's voice as she struggled to speak. She was coughing and having to take breaths in between every couple of words. I felt so helpless. My mother was calling out to me but I didn't know how to help her. Tears raced down my face but I knew I had to be strong for her. We ended up talking on the phone for an hour. We talked about any and everything except my problems.

When we got off the phone, I started packing my things to go back home. A couple of my teammates came over when they heard the news. They helped me pack as well. I didn't say much. The last of my worries at the time was school. And the thought of possibly going back to jail for violation of probation was still lingering until later that week. I left the school but I had to come back to get the rest of my things. When I got back, my coach had some good news for me. Coach G told me that my charges weren't going to be criminal charges. The university was the one actually pulling my scholarship. This meant no jail time, but I still couldn't play basketball. Then he told me that there were some boosters, also known as old alumni from the school, who were willing to pay my tuition. Then I could continue with school and play as a walk on. I thought about it, but decided against it. I decided against it because I knew that if the word got out about boosters paying my tuition for the rest of the year, it would backfire on me. Besides, after finding out that it was the university pulling my scholarship, I didn't want to be there just as much as they didn't want me there!

VI

After doing some research and wanting to be closer to Lorraine, I ended up transferring to a mid-major in Tennessee. It was closer to home and I didn't have to sit out after transferring.

Instead, I had to wait until the next semester started. I didn't really care because there was only a month left in the semester. The coaching staff found me a spot to stay and enrolled me in classes but I had to pay for all that shit myself. My scholarship wasn't going to kick in until the next year since I transferred mid semester. That meant I had to pay out of state tuition and rent.

I had some money left over from my last situation with my old school, but that was just enough for the down payment. After paying tuition and the first and last month's rent, $3,000 was gone real quick! I only had $1,500 left to my name and the next payment installments were due in one month. I had to think of something, fast! I was stressed out daily. I figured after the coaching staff saw me play, I could at least get some more time to pay, but I couldn't play until the next semester started. Finals and winter break was almost a six week span and all of it was hitting me at once. There were a couple people from my old high school at this university who knew about my situation and wanted to take me out. I, on the other hand, wanted to keep a low profile, so going out wasn't a priority. Besides, the last time I went out, I almost got locked back up. But after much convincing, I gave in and we went out; I knew I needed to get out to see how the school and parties operated anyway.

Since I transferred mid-semester, all the classes were locked so I could only take online courses. That meant I never really had to step foot on campus until practice started. The campus was totally different from my last. It was a lot smaller but they partied a lot harder! Once again, there wasn't a professional team here, so all the good colleges got all of the extra attention. This was a basketball area in general, surrounded by the top programs like Kentucky, Louisville, Memphis, and Tennessee. I always saw their players at the same parties because the area was so small. My school was in a dry county and people literally had to drive at least 45 minutes to the next county or city just to get liquor for the parties. They also smoked the worst weed ever. I mean at best, it was mid-grade.

Right before we went out one night, I saw the hassle a couple of my friends went through just to get some bullshit ass weed. I looked at it once they bought it and the bag had all kinds of seeds in it. They were smoking mids and I knew I could get some kush from back home. And then it hit me.

I could sell weed up here to pay my rent and tuition. It was just a thought at first but the more I thought about it, the more it made sense.

Finals were almost over and winter break was starting. That meant everybody was going to be partying! Atlanta was only three hours away so I drove home to get the weed myself. Plus I didn't have all the money so I needed to talk to some people face to face.

The first person I went to talk to was Knowledge! He was out of jail and I knew he was connected because he used to sell weed when we were locked up together. Knowledge was a solid nigga. I trusted him. He remembered the favors I used to do for him when we were locked up so he let me get a whole pound for free. I ended up giving him $1,000 anyway so he knew that the money was no problem for me. I had to pay tuition and rent for another semester so I wanted to make sure he knew I was going to be coming back.

Before I went back to school, I picked up Brandon and Corey. It was a small town and word spread quick there. Of course I didn't want people to know it was me with the weed, so I brought my homeboys to help me get it off. Half of it was already sold; They were just waiting for me to get it back to Tennessee. I let Brandon and Corey know the situation along the ride so by the time we got there they were already ready to go. After almost two weeks, we met our quota. I was able to pay my rent and my second tuition installment. I made sure Knowledge got the three stacks I owed him and I also paid Brandon and Corey for the help. They were pocketing all their money because they were either staying with me or kicking it with some girls they had met. I was happy they were there helping and also happy I was able to help them out.

Finals were over and winter break had started. I could finally practice with the team.

Everybody went home for winter break, so outside of the locals and the athletes, the school was empty as hell. The down time allowed me to get cool with some baseball players. Believe it or not, they were the wildest ones at the school. Tyler, the shortstop, I called him Zack Morris. He was always into some shit it seemed like, so finding out he was a plug came of no surprise.

Ecstasy pills was his hustle. He was the one supplying all these crazy ass rave and frat parties. Zach came from money and his family was very well off. Zach's father was a former MLB player and his mother was a former Olympic track star. Zack rolled around campus in a clean ass drop top black Porsche. The tags read "DEEZ NUTS". We got cool over an awkward conversation of how he got his best weed ever in Atlanta. My antennas were up. I just wanted to hear him out.

Zack wasn't really interested in the weed but he did speak more openly about the pills. "This shit is a fucking gold mine! I buy five hundred pills for $15 a pill and come here and sell them for $20 a pill. I re-up every weekend, four times a month." He was a little drunk, so I didn't know if he was telling the truth. I decided to pick his brain a little more.

"Damn Zack, that's like 10 racks a month! If you eating like that then I need to put you on to my cousin."

He shrugged. "Nahhhh. I like things how they are. The more people you deal with, the more risk you take."

His serious demeanor led me to believe he was telling the truth. I knew if he wasn't going to work with me that I was going to cut his ass out, but that was just a matter of time. Zach was selling regular ecstasy pills but I had access to triple stacks. They were just a stronger version of the ecstasy Zach was selling. At that time, pills weren't selling like that back home because people had other recreational drugs. So since the demand was low, I knew I could get them for cheap.

My drawback was I didn't want to become a drug dealer or even be looked at in any other cliche. I honestly just needed the money and this seemed like the quickest way. I was basically just going to get Brandon and Corey to supply the suppliers. That was my whole plan. That way, we wouldn't have to do any leg work and things could just stay the same. Everybody could keep their same clientele and nobody had to know it was me supplying. It was a good plan and all the numbers added up.

After about two weeks of planning and preparation, I set it up for Knowledge to front me two pounds of kush and my cousin in Detroit gave me 500 triple stacks. I was getting the weed for $250 an ounce but selling it for $500 an ounce so basically I was doubling my money. One pound would pay Knowledge and the other was all profit. Since I was supplying the actual dealers, I only broke it down to all ounces. This made the sales very easy. There were no negotiations with the prices: $500 for an ounce, $2,000 for a quarter, $4,000 for a half, and $8,000 for the whole thing. When you have the best product, you can charge what you want. I set the market.

Knowledge fronted me 500 more triple stacks. It was like a trial run. We both wanted to see if we could make something happen with the pills. Even though he gave them to me for free, he charged me $5 per pill on the turnaround. That was still only $2,005. I got Brandon and Corey to sell the pills around campus for $25 per pill. That was a $20 profit. After getting all the pills off, I made about $12,500. I paid Knowledge his $2,500 for the pills and I also gave him the $8,000 for the two pounds. Even though it took a little longer to get the pills off, I walked away with about 18 stacks profit. I gave Brandon and Corey $4,000 a piece and kept the remaining $10,000 for myself. That gave me a little financial comfort because my bills and tuition in total came up to about $3,000 per month.

Nobody knew it was me that had all this mastermind dealing going on and that's how I wanted to keep it. People had to talk directly to Brandon or

Corey before it got to me. Other students just thought that Brandon and Corey were my cousins and up at the school to watch games and holla at the girls. It was a great disguise. Especially when they both started talking to two girls on the dance team.

Basketball picked back up and I was doing good. I ended up averaging over 18 points my first three games. I also averaged six assists so I was definitely working the ball with the tam.

Our first rivalry game was the day I made my mark at the school. I didn't know it was a rivalry, so I approached it like any other game. It was an away game and the crowd was super intense! I'd been in environments like this before, so it wasn't a big deal to me. As we warmed up for the game, there was a group of people that kept calling my name to get my attention. Initially I didn't look or pay them any mind, but my teammates came over and told me what was going on. There was a group of people in one section who had on orange jumpsuits. They stood out because their school colors were blue and yellow. They all had my last name on the back of their sweat suits.

Of course I didn't catch on to the joke at first until I saw some other students with white and black pinstripe sweat suits on with my last name on the back. They were all calling me a convict and dressed like inmates.

I actually don't even know how they knew I went to prison, but this shit got under my skin! I mean they had props like handcuffs and all. Yelling things on the court like "don't drop the soap!" It was very creative; I'll give them that. But them heckling me still really pissed me off!

It got to me because the people making those jokes were some country ass racist folks. They really didn't give a damn about the game. They just wanted to aggravate me and get under my skin.

A couple of them were escorted out by the police for throwing beer on the court right on me. Whenever I would give them the satisfaction of looking over their way, they would throw up their middle finger and make all types of obscene gestures. I went back to the locker room before the game started to change my jersey because my original jersey was soaked from the beer that was thrown on me. As I walked out of the tunnel, escorted by my coach and a real police officer, I was called all types of nigger and racial slurs. Neither my coach nor the police officer said anything. They just gave me that look.

As soon as the game started, I took all of my frustrations out on their team. I didn't even remember getting tired. I finished the game with 32 points, 11 rebounds, 7 assists, and 3 steals. I only played 30 minutes because we blew their team out by 20 points. I never looked in their direction let alone gave them any of my time.

After the game, the same people in the same section with those same jumpsuits on asked me for my autograph. I just kept walking and didn't respond. I was still on strike from all media and refused to do any interviews. When we got back to school, I was the talk of the campus. That made it a little more difficult to keep a low profile, still nobody knew what I was doing to survive.

After about a month, it was time to get some more money. Everyone had sold out of all the weed they had and were getting calls about more. Brandon and Corey told me how a couple of people we were getting it to wanted more. I didn't really care about the weed, it was the pills that had my interest! I knew Zach was the man when it came down to that ecstasy clientele so I needed him on the team. I invited him over one night to try the weed I had. It was the same kush I was selling everybody else, I just wanted to talk to him face to face. I made it seem like it was my cousins, Brandon and Corey, who could get him the pills for $10 per pill. That was $5 less than what he was paying so it was going to be more profit. I even convinced him to sell them for

$25 instead of $20. It was also convenient because Zach could just get the pills from Brandon and Corey instead of going out of town. Less risk, more reward!

Instead of 500 pills this time, I went home and got 1,000. I got them for $5 a pill and sold them to Zach for $10 a pill. Zach only bought 500 at first to see how they were going to sell.

Little did he know, we had already sold some triple stacks around campus before and they were coming back for more. Once we sold Zach his 500 pills, I put that $5,000 up immediately. That was Knowledge's money. I told Brandon and Corey to sell the other 500 pills for $25 per pill. After a week, Zach came right back. He needed 500 more pills so I went back home to get more. I never took Brandon and Corey with me to meet Knowledge; The less they knew, the better it was for me. I didn't mind the drive because I knew I was going to double my money every time. Knowledge would give me 1,000 pills for $5,000 and I would sell 500 pills to Zach for $5,000. I would have Brandon and Corey sell the other 500 pills for $25 per pill. This meant that Zach was basically paying my debt to Knowledge with the 500 pills he purchased and the other 500 pills were all profit! At $25 per pill, I was making $12,500 off of the other 500 pills. I would let Brandon and Corey split $2,500 and I would keep $10,000 to myself. That might seem a bit extreme, but it was my money and my connect. I just had Brandon and Corey working for me because I trusted them. They were both making about $5,000 per month anyway and the pills were selling themselves. It was easy work if you ask me.

Things became routine and almost two months had passed. Financially, I was comfortable and school was going great. I had a 3.5 grade point average and I really didn't even apply myself. My classes weren't that hard, they were just time consuming. I spent most of my time in class thinking about all the other shit I had going on outside of school. I was up to making almost 40 stacks a month. After paying tuition and rent, I would take home about $35,000 a month.

Things were moving too damn fast in that slow town, so I decided to slow down and stop. Quitting while you're ahead is always something people fail to do in these situations, but not me. I wasn't in it for the lifestyle, just for the money. As a student athlete, the hardest thing in the world to do was to keep a low profile, especially since the team was doing so well.

From the time I arrived to the beginning of the NCAA tournament, we had only lost three games. Every home game was sold out and the fans even traveled with us on the road. We were the talk of Tennessee and quickly became the team to beat. After advancing to the second round of the NCAA tournament, we lost in overtime. I never believed in moral victories, but I guess they did because our fan base grew even more after the tournament. There were only two seniors on the team, so we were returning 10 players. That along with the 21 points and 6 assists I averaged as a freshman gave us a top 25 ranking the following season.

I started hearing talks of me being an NBA prospect the next season. That was even more reason for me to chill out. On the other hand, after all the difficulties I had been through in college, I didn't pay the NBA rumors any attention and my no media strike was still going hard.

It wasn't until the head coach sat me down before preseason started that I took the rumors serious.

"King, ya know, the people who are questioning your abilities aren't questioning your talent. But they're questioning your character! What type of person is he off the court? What is his work ethic? Is he on time? Is he a leader? All questions leading up to can he be responsible if we were to invest in YOU!"

"Well who's asking these questions coach?"

"People on the next level. They're asking me because I hold your future in my hands." My coach really didn't like me. He usually went out of his way to be an asshole. You see, he didn't recruit me. I was considered a walk on transfer after getting into that drama at Alabama Tech. Then I just kind of came over and became the face of the program. Since the success of the program was literally securing his future, you would think he would be happy for me. Instead, this man acted like it was a bad thing that I was playing so well.

In that short amount of time, we only had a player-coach relationship. Meaning, outside of basketball, we never ever spoke. I used to think him holding me in drills and practice was just him trying to push me, until I realized it was personal. He would make me go to study hall even though I had a 3.5 GPA and then go out of his way to ask the assistant coaches in front of the whole team, 'did King go to study hall?' Of course there were other players on the team who had lower GPAs who didn't have to go to study hall. Just dumb shit. He even made me attend summer school that year. When I got there, it was only me and the three freshman he signed.

Coach also made me get another car because he said mine was too flashy for a college athlete. That was the type of petty shit I was dealing with so you could imagine the look on my face when he said he had my future in his hands.

I responded in my usual sarcastic tone. "Well coach, I'm assuming these are professionals since you said next level. And if they are professionals, I'm sure they can get those answers. I just expect you like I would expect anyone else to just simply tell the truth. And my future is never in your hands, you're just my coach!"

He kicked me out of his office, but it wasn't a big deal.

My mother passed away right before the season started, so my little brother had to stay with me. After paying for the funeral arrangements, I still had a good amount of money left over. I was finally back on my scholarship funds, so the stress of paying tuition and rent was over.

Things were becoming routine again and seemed normal. My grades were straight, I had money in my pocket, and basketball was taking care of itself. Usually when things were going this good, some bullshit was right around the corner so I was expecting it. This time it came in the form of a phone call.

"King! I fucked up, I fucked up bad, my nigga!" It was my brother calling from prison.

"I need you to come see me in prison!"

His tone was so uneasy and tensed so I knew shit was serious. I needed to go visit him but that was going to be tough with my hectic school and basketball schedule. My days were full and we were in season. I thought about it and said fuck it and left to go see him anyway. This just so happened to be game day, so I was pushing it. He was locked up in Alabama State Prison which was a convenient hour and a half away. I left early in the morning so I could be back by shoot around.

When I finally got there and saw him, he had a deep scar on his neck, bandages on his ribs from being stabbed three times, and bruises on his face. He said what's up with a slur that's when I realized his jaw was wired shut.

A tear rolled down my eye.

"Don't cry for me, my nigga, I'm still breathing!"

That immediately put things into perspective because I knew what prison was like. My brother told me there was a bounty on his head because he set up a drug deal that went bad. He had his people meet up with some Dominicans to get some heroin, and they ended up dropping the Dominicans, leaving behind a $100,000 mess that they held him responsible for. I was the only one on the outside that he had in his corner, but I damn sure didn't have 100 racks to clean this mess up.

I eventually made it back to shoot around just in time for Coach to tell me I was late. After some extra and excessive running and smart ass comments threatening to not start me in that night's game, I headed to the locker room. I was distant from everybody the whole day and ended up having a mediocre ass game. I only had 8 points, 3 assists, and 3 turnovers.

That was hands down my worst college game yet. I knew that each second that pass with time against my brother's life, and those thoughts consumed me and were definitely responsible for my shitty performance on the court. I couldn't even eat. The look on his face was a burned image in my head.

I ended up staying up for two nights straight which caused me to dehydrate. I went to the ER and I just sat there with IV's in my arm and it hit me. I knew I could come up with $100,000 because I damn near made that in two months the year before. I just didn't have that amount of time to spare. I needed time to come up with that paper and I knew just who to call.

Desperate times call for desperate measures. My plan was to reach out to El Capo! I knew that he could get in touch with the Dominicans and call off the hit by either paying them or at least buying me some time. In an ideal world, El Capo would pay off the $100,000 to the Dominicans. And over a period of time, I would work on paying El Capo back. The only problem was, I didn't know how to get in touch with him. The only person who did was Knowledge.

Knowledge gave me his mailing address in prison and I wrote him a letter. In the letter, I just reminded El Capo of who I was and where I was at. I told him about school and all that and I also asked for him to put me on his visitation list so I could talk to him face to face. El Capo respected me because of how I carried myself in prison.

He agreed to meet with me, but once again, I had to find time with my crazy ass basketball and school schedule. I ended up lying and saying I had a funeral to go to since the only time I could visit El Capo was on a Wednesday.

When I walked into the jail, I started having flashbacks of when I was in prison. It was the same jail. The only thing that had changed was time. All of the same faces from the guards to the inmates made me nervous about my own fucking situation. One false move and I was right back in that miserable motherfucker! I found logic and reason in what I was doing by telling myself that if I do get caught, at least I would actually be guilty this time! Wrong thing for the right reason. The security guard escorted me to meet El Capo just like they did a couple years ago. I walked in and this nigga was still living just as good. We shook hands firmly and sat down.

"You come bearing gifts, you must need a favor." El Capo said.

During our firm handshake, I gave him the cell phone I managed to sneak past security. Prior to our meeting, I gave one of the correction officers $1,000 to bring in the phone. It was easy to sneak it past the guards because I had been locked up before, so I had a couple tricks up my sleeve. We only had 15 minutes, so I had to make the conversation quick.

I told El Capo in as much detail as I could what was going on.

"What's happening, big dog! My brother got into it with the Dominicans. You know it's serious if I came all the way down here to see you face to face. Anyway, he called a play from behind the wall for some dog food. Then without him knowing, his people threw a surprise party! To make a long story short, it's a whole hun dun on his head and he already locked up! I actually got a way to come up 100 racks, but not in the Dominican's short time frame. I was wondering if you could do what you do and I pay the 100 bands to you in installments over the next year. That way my brother will be safe and make it home, and you'll get your monthly quota from me."

El Capo didn't even ask me what I had going on. He just looked at me with a blank nonchalant stare and said, "Let me think about it!" We shook hands and I went on about my business. I wasn't trying to be in there any longer than I had to be.

I got a letter three days later from a third party that said 'consider it done'. It also had the account number to deposit the money. That's when I knew it was on. The best part was that timing couldn't be any better because I had just received an $8,000 Pell Grant check from the school. I filed as an independent and let them know I was supporting my 10 year old brother so they gave me the full amount for one semester. Since I had a full athlete scholarship, my tuition and books were already paid. They even paid for my new apartment off of campus. So I was able to take that $1,000 and put it to the side for El Capo.

I knew it was going to take a little more time to get shit moving because Zach had graduated. That weekly loss caused me to have to put my own face card on things and do some leg work myself. By that time, everybody around Tennessee knew me, so I knew who to get it to. Same route as last time, supply the suppliers. Only this go round, we were moving the weed and the pills at the same time. Business Administration was my major and I had my own business on the side. I still managed to maintain a 3.5 GPA or higher and averaged 22 points, 6 assists, and 5 rebounds per game.

After paying El Capo monthly, I profited about $20,000 dollars a month. It was easy to manage these things because of my different personalities. Who I was on the court was totally different from who I was off the court. There was an even bigger difference in my personality in the classroom.

As we headed towards March Madness again, we had only lost two games. Some NBA teams had me going top 25 in the upcoming draft, and some had me going second round. It's hard to pay the NBA any attention when you have so much other real life shit going on. I couldn't think past the month. I wanted March to be all about basketball so my focus was on the tournament. I was up a little bit so I could afford to take the month off. Brandon and Corey were eating pretty good too, but wanted more money on some greedy shit. Corey wanted to be a Kingpin and Brandon just followed suit. Corey asked for one of my connects since he knew I was taking the whole month off. I didn't know what got into that nigga! He just fell in love with the life I guess. I have some with the call and he just fell in love with the action. I refused to give this nigga the connect as he constantly blew my phone up on the road. He was constantly talking wreckless through text mentioning things that we only knew about. So I blocked his number.

My only focus was basketball and we had Syracuse the first round. After watching film, I saw that Syracuse played a zone defense and I knew exactly how to attack them. I was the focus of attention from my squad, so I wanted to get everybody aggressively involved.

From the opening tip of the game, I saw quick double teams and made the correct passes. My teammates seemed nervous. Maybe it was the bright lights. We went into halftime down 10 points. I only had 4 of them. I was making the correct passes but we were missing all the open shots. Coach didn't even care. I was the leader of my team so he chewed my ass out!

"King, I'm gonna start calling your ass Prince! Scouts talking all this shit about you ready for the NBA. We can't even get past the first round! Let me tell you something, son, the whole world is watching! You're supposed to be the best so you have to be that all the time! And that goes for the rest of you too. Find a way! As for not getting any calls, we're the fucking underdogs! We haven't did shit yet! This is a fuckin' mid-major versus a huge division one school. Why would you be getting calls? Some of you seniors," he pointed at them. "This could easily be your last game. And it's no guarantee you're going to make it to the next level so you might have to get a job! And to the so-called "stars" of this team, your draft stock will go down as others who's still playin' and leadin' their team will continue to go up. Do you know that you guys are a fucking 20-to-1 underdog in the paper today? Think about it. 20-to-1 odds. That's what the world thinks of you right now. And to be honest, y'all er' out there looking like the odds shoulda been higher. In favor Syracuse! If you don't want to fuckin' play, I'll start my freshman and recruit better when the season is over!"

Then he walked out.

Initially I was pissed off! Thinking to myself, does this nigga know I only took two shots and I made both of them? But then I snapped out of it and heard what coach said loud and clear. This was just his fucked up way to get us motivated.

Since I stood in the forefront, he targeted me. I wanted my troops to know I had their back, so I spoke.

"I want to apologize fellas. I was very passive and not as aggressive as I normally am. I knew that they were going to try to get the ball out of my hands, so I was trying to get y'all open shots. I'm going to tell coach to move me to the two so it can free me up. This game is far from over. They gave us their best shot and they only up to 10. Not to mention we ain't hit shit the first half and I ain't even got off yet. We going to win this game, fellas, or we're going to lose this bitch fighting! Trust me. We gotta trust each other like we've been doing all year! There's a reason we only lost two games this season. This ain't no fuckin Cinderella story, fellas, we belong here! And we damn sure ain't no underdogs. Syracuse ain't even ranked! I've been to the so-called big school. We all know my story. And we work just as hard, if not harder, than they do. This is a test of will. You stand up and piss like the next man! Ain't nothin' to be nervous about unless you scared to be great!" I could sense their hype rising so I got even more intense. "These are the times you're going to remember for the rest of your life. Embrace it!! Just like we had to embrace losing last year. I know you all remember the feeling. Let's just have fun. Take it back to your AAU days. Remember that feeling. Bring that same energy and we'll be aight.

Come on, bring it in. Ain't nothin' else to talk about. Let's get it on 3. 1, 2, 3 let's get it!"

We came out the gates firing! We went on a 12 and 2 run, tying the game immediately.

They called a timeout and we had the crowd going! The momentum shifted our way. Right out of the time out, we got a quick steal and dunk off of a missed shot, followed by two quick threes from me. Before we knew it, I had the hot hand. I did everything in my power to keep the crowd going and the momentum in our favor.

After a couple crazy crossovers, a couple dunks, some fancy passes, I was hands down the best player on the court! We won that game by 12 points. I finished with 16 points and 16 assists, setting the new school record for most assists in my school's history of being in the tournament. The scouting report on me before this game was that I was just a prolific scorer, so finishing with 16 assists was definitely going to help my draft status.

Our next game wasn't for a couple days. I definitely was becoming even more of a household name in the post-game interviews. I decided to come off my media strike because I knew I was nothing like the media portrayed me in the past. My witty personality and sarcastic comebacks made me popular.

Lorraine and I had lost contact when she went off to grad school. She knew I hated the media and she knew exactly why. So when I saw her at the press conference seemed like fate, her being there for my first interview.

I purposely gave dry and subtle answers before finally pointing right to Lorraine to ask me a question.

"King! You definitely seem like the crown holder tonight leading your team past Syracuse! Your first and second half performance seemed like two totally different players. Can you explain what got into you??"

Then, with a straight face, knowing that the whole sports world was watching, I said, "Well, Lorraine, here's the deal. I'm the best there is plain and simple, ya know. I mean, I wake up in the morning and I piss excellence. Nobody can hang with my stuff. If you ain't first, you are last!"

Of course I said it in a joking manner, but my comeback was so quick and straight faced that some of the media didn't catch the sarcasm. That was a direct quote from one of my favorite movies. We had actually watched it on the bus ride to a couple of games. My teammates all burst out laughing including Coach. I was pretty sure the media was going to take that out of context, but I didn't much care. That interview went viral. People were making highlight tapes of the game with my interview playing in the background on YouTube. I was becoming an even bigger household name overnight.

The storyline was getting even better because we had to play my former school Alabama Tech next. We got our ass kicked last year in the second round and that shit hurt. I remembered that pain vividly. This game was personal and I wasn't going to waste any time being aggressive!

My coaches knew the history and what this game meant to me so they let me loose. They called the first five plays for me and I came out of the gates firing. I was so anxious to bust their ass that I missed all five shots. The whole team was definitely fucking with me hard that day because they still called the next play for me.

That's when it happened. Alabama Tech was in a matchup zone defense. I'm guessing because of the success that Syracuse had against us the game before. We overlooked the ball to one side, and threw a skip pass to me. I was open for the shot, but fumbled the pass a little bit. This allowed them to recover but they were scrambling. I dribbled to the top of the key when I noticed the shot clock at six seconds. I called for a screen and split the defense up top. That's when everything went in slow motion. As I split the screen, he rolled to the basket. I got to about the free throw line and I threw the ball up. The defender thought I was passing to my teammate rolling to the basket, so he kind of shaded towards him. They turned around to box out for the rebound, but I had thrown the ball to myself off the backboard. By the time he realized it, I was already in mid-air. I don't even know what made me do that crazy shit, it was just a reflexive reaction. I caught the ball off the glass and dunked it so hard!

I was yelling and hanging on the rim, pointing to my old coach while I was still on the rim. The refs gave me a technical foul of course, but the reactions of the fans was crazy. Not only did I steal the momentum of the crowd, but that play also took Alabama Tech's heart. I could see it in the defenders' eyes. They couldn't fuck with me at all! This game was all personal, forget business.

They tried double teaming me, but that didn't work. I found other ways to dominate the game because I already expected that. Coach G did a great job preparing us because the game was close all the way to the last minute. We only won by 6 point, but I put up some fucking PlayStation numbers! I finished with 31 points, 12 rebounds, 8 assists, 5 steals, and 3 blocks. I also played the whole 40 minutes with only one foul. And that was from the technical when I was hanging on the rim.

After the game, we were supposed to shake hands. Instead, I walked over to our fans that were in the crowd. They couldn't storm the court because there was another tournament game going on after ours, but that didn't stop them from celebrating right there where they were. Of course I knew the cameras were on me, but I didn't care. The university shitted on me while I was there, so I didn't want to touch anybody's hand! Not even Coach G's. Like I said, it was all personal.

After showering and getting dressed, I had to address the media. Once again, I gave all one word answers until I saw Lorraine.

"King, what were some of your thoughts after starting the game 0 and 5? It seems like you got yourself going after that amazing play throwing the ball off the backward to yourself. What was going through your mind?"

As soon as Lorraine finished talking I quickly replied. I actually already knew she was going to ask that question. I replied promptly in a very serious tone.

"I wanted to embarrass them. I'm talking about public humiliation against the whole team like the university did me. This game was definitely personal given our history. I just want to thank my current coaching staff and teammates for understanding how much this game meant to me. Nothing was going through my mind actually. I was just free. I think I was a little too anxious when the game first started. So naturally, I had to calm my nerves. I didn't even sleep last night because I wanted to play so bad! When I threw the ball off the backboard to myself that was just me improvising. It was more of a spur of the moment type of play. I didn't know exactly what I was doing even though it looked planned and happened really fast. Everything was in slow motion for me though."

"Did you have any words for your former coach or teammates after the game?" Lorraine asked.

"No, not really," I shook my head. "It really wasn't much to say. I mean, I talked to some of the guys on Facebook here and there, I do wish them the best though."

I downplayed how I really felt about the school and program because I didn't want my comments to overshadow the fact that we won the game. We were headed to the Sweet 16 for the first time in over 30 years. My draft stock was at an all-time high. After that game, agents from multiple agencies went out of their way to get in touch with me. The NBA was projecting me to be a top 10 lottery pick. I was finally realizing that my dreams could really become a reality.

We had a whole week before our next game, so I decided to check on Brandon and Corey to see what was really going on. After all that shit Corey was talking through text, I just wanted to go check this nigga's temperature. I didn't even let them know I was back in town, I just pulled up to one of our spots and saw them outside. I didn't say a word, I just got out of the car and punch this nigga right in his nose. We fought for a while, before Brandon broke it up. He ran towards his car. I knew exactly what he was going to do; I just wanted to see if he had enough balls to do it!

Corey went and grabbed his gun. I didn't have anything on me but a knife, but the chances of me stabbing him were a lot higher than him shooting me. Brandon knew that. Brandon ran towards Corey trying to hold him back and calm him down.

I told that nigga straight up.

"Aye my nigga, if you pull that mother fucker out, you better use it! Cause you know it's only $2,500 to get you marked! You work for me and I pay you more than that so that shit won't be an issue!

Corey just looked at me in total shock. He sucked his teeth in total disgust.

"I've known you my whole damn life, bruh, and this is how you treat me? The godfather of my daughter!"

"Daughter!?" I yelled. "Nigga, what you talking about? Brandon, what this nigga talking about!?"

Nobody told me that Corey had a daughter on the way.

"You mother fucker! With who?? The same chick you been fuckin' with? Damn, how many months?"

Corey's girl was six months pregnant. That's why he was trippin so hard the past couple of weeks. Not only was he scared and nervous about having his first child, but he was also scared and nervous because there was a good chance the baby was going to be born prematurely.

Corey's girl had a disorder called Renal Disease. I didn't know much about the disease except that it was a dysfunction of the kidneys due to low blood flow to the kidneys. The doctors told them that there was an 85 percent chance of having the baby prematurely. Corey was stressed the fuck out! Not only about his child and baby mother's condition, but her parents were unaccepting of him too. They didn't approve of their daughter talking to a black guy. I had always found that really weird, because her mother was black! After hearing all of that shit, I felt exactly where he was coming from. He couldn't take any time off. They weren't under insurance so he was paying all the medical bills out of pocket.

I decided to put together another play with Knowledge. Knowledge and I always met face to face, but since we were in the tournament, I didn't have time to leave. I also had to play catch up in school. Some of my professors worked with me because they knew about the rigorous athlete schedule, but some thought we were over privileged and went out of their way to be extra for no damn reason.

I called Knowledge to get my normal package but this time I had Corey go meet him halfway. I told him to have somebody meet Corey at a Walmart parking lot which was about an hour and a half away. Knowledge was skeptical at first, but after I told him why, he agreed.

The plan was simple. Meet in the parking lot, count the money, make sure the weed was completely sealed and not tampered with and make sure he counted all the pills. I chose the Walmart parking lot because it was a public place in mid-day, so there was going to be a lot of traffic. That way nothing would look suspicious. We left around noon to make the pick-up. I had school and practice so I wasn't expecting to see Corey until around 7 p.m. that night. I knew it would take him about four hours to get there and get back. On my way to practice, Corey texted me, letting me know everything was cool and he was on his way back. I figured everything was straight and I would see him after study hall.

Then night time rolls around, and this nigga was nowhere to be found.

I didn't panic, instead I called Brandon to see if he knew where he was. Brandon didn't know either.

"I talked to him about two or three hours ago. I haven't heard from him since. Maybe he's at the hospital with his girl and the baby."

I thought to myself, *maybe you're right, but then again, why would you go to the hospital with all that work in the car?* Any normal person would have at least dropped it off. I mean, he had a key to my apartment. They both did. Something didn't make sense. After finally reaching out to his girlfriend, we realized that nobody talked to him for the past two hours. That's when I started to panic!

Shit was going too smooth and too routine for this all of a sudden disappearing shit.

Something happened and I needed to find out what.

I called Knowledge to make sure he got all his money. I definitely didn't want those problems. Knowledge was cool and everything was everything on his end. The money got there safely which meant that Corey still had the package. Corey was too stupid to run off with my package. I mean, where was he even going to sell it at? The gold mine was literally around the campus. There was no way he could make those moves around here without me knowing so I scratched that thought. The weed he picked up wasn't even going for the same prices back home as they were in Tennessee, so I knew he didn't take it back home. The pills wouldn't have even sold back home either, so I knew there was more to the story. I gave Corey the benefit of the doubt, but my patience wore thin as the night went on.

That night, I went to sleep and had a crazy ass dream. I don't know if it was déjà vu, but that shit felt real. I can't remember exactly what happened, but I do remember things happening in sequences in my dream. Like a domino effect. It was like if I made one decision in my dream, I could actually see all the events that would happen as a result of making that decision. It was weird because it felt like I could actually see and feel my decisions playing out right in front of me.

I woke up and went on about my day as usual. Still nobody had heard from Corey. I grew more and more worried as the day went by. Two days turned into a week. A whole fucking week! I wasn't focused in practice at all, gearing up for the Sweet 16. Shit, I couldn't remember who we were even playing next.

I played every scenario out in my head and none of them added up. Corey was one of my closest friends in the world. I wasn't completely opposed to the fact that he could have run off with the package, but I just couldn't see him doing that. I mean this nigga had a baby on the way and I was paying him well. I even knew his parents. It just didn't make sense why he would throw everything away. I wanted to tell Knowledge, but I didn't want him getting all nervous and thinking I didn't have my situation under control. I decided to keep it to myself.

As we got ready to play UCLA in the Sweet 16, I wasn't there mentally at all. The repercussions of what would happen if I didn't get El Capo his paper consumed me. They for sure would have killed my brother and me. This is a big dog we're talking about. El fucking Capo! The same nigga living better in prison than people are on the street. I needed to come up with a plan and I needed to come up with a plan real quick.

That's when it hit me. All this thinking about El Capo helped me remember how much of a gambler he actually was. I remember when I was locked up, I set the sports line and was getting money in prison. Since we were a mid-major basketball team, the odds were against us the whole tournament. That meant that if I placed a sports bet on us, I could win some money real quick. I wasn't looking to win a lot, just enough to pay El Capo that month.

The odds against us playing UCLA were 10-to-1, so if I put down $1,000, I could win $10,000 back. I told Brandon to let me hold $1,000, but I didn't tell him why. I just wanted to give him his $1,000 back after we won. I just knew that $2,000 with 10-to-1 odds would put me right where I needed to be. Nobody needed to know what I was doing, so I placed that bet through an online site in Vegas. I had a dummy name on a rush card, but it was a real account and an official online gambling site.

Now all I needed to do was win the game!

Pressure at this point in my life wasn't a big deal, it was just something to deal with. In the meantime, nobody had heard shit from Corey!

UCLA was better than us, straight up. They knew it, we knew it, and our coaching staff even knew it. Before the game started, instead of giving us a motivational speech, this nigga was telling us how we had a good run this year. Little did they know, I had $20,000 on this game and a hit on my head if I couldn't come up with this money. Fuck what they were talking about, we had to win! UCLA had seven players projected to go to the NBA and they were the favorites to win the tournament. The only reason the odds were 10-to-1 was because they knew I was a fucking problem.

No, I'm joking!

The reason the odds were 10-to-1 was because my school was ironically hosting the Sweet 16 tournament that year. The NCAA randomly selected schools to host games in the tournament. Given how the 64 team bracket went, there was no way to predict us to have a home game in the tournament. This was pure fate! It felt like it was destined to happen.

As I ran out of the tunnel and took the court, I caught myself in a daze. I was staring into the crowd, and everything just went mute. As I looked at the faces and tuned out the noise, all I could think to myself was damn, I came a long way! These people didn't know my struggle, and they damn sure didn't know what I was going through. They didn't have to though, because I was here! I wanted to embrace every moment, because I knew it could all be taken away just like that.

I said a prayer for the first time in a while during the national anthem.

"Father..." Then I apologized for about two minutes.

As I prayed, a sequence of events of my past flashed in my brain. It was like a time line, leading up to this point. Tears rolled down my eyes, these vivid images of my past covered my thoughts. I could feel my thoughts and emotions changing. All the people who told me I couldn't, all the obstacles and diversities I had to overcome, all the pain I had to endure, it was all me. A perfect imperfection. Orchestrated chaos. As I got back into my prayer, all I could say was thank you.

I guess God heard me loud and clear on this prayer because I went crazy that game.

Everything was just flowing freely. I was relaxed and didn't feel any pressure. I hadn't had fun like that since I was practicing *NBA Inside Stuff* highlights with my brothers as a kid. The game was fairly close, but I was poised till the very end. I didn't miss a single shot and went a perfect 9 for 9 from the field. UCLA tied the game up at the end with a desperation 3 pointer, sending the game into its first overtime. Since they had matchup problems, they switched their defense to a zone.

That's when I knew I had them.

I told my teammates to let me create a play for them and be ready to knock shots down. That's exactly what they did. As I broke the zone defense down and passed the ball out to them, they knocked down some big shots. UCLA had to burn two quick timeouts and come out of the zone defense. That's when I took it upon myself to take us home. Until that point in overtime, I hadn't taken a shot; I just created plays for my teammates. When they switched back to a man to man defense, I scored 6 points, straight sealing the victory! The crowd stormed the court. This was the first time in over 30 years my school was going to the Elite 8. The looks on my teammates' faces were priceless.

It hadn't hit me yet that we just pulled off one of the biggest upsets in NCAA history. I didn't know what to feel. On one hand, I was in complete disbelief and on the other I was worried about my home boy Corey.

I was numb, there I was supposed to be enjoying my once in a lifetime feeling I had other shit on my mind. Twenty bands was definitely enough to get me over, but it still wasn't 100. I owed El Capo about $50,000 more. I hated feeling the way I did. It was like two big ass clouds hanging over my head. I was so tired of living my life like this. All the worry. All the stress. All the drama. All of it. When I got back to the locker room, I had a couple of missed phone callsand texts. They were both from Brandon and Corey's girlfriend. I called Brandon first to see what was up.

He told me that he heard from Corey.

"King, I just talked to bruh. He called me from jail! Since we switch numbers so much, he couldn't get in touch with us. I don't know his angle, but he sound super nervous! He told me he got pulled over with everything!"

I cut Brandon off right there. "What jail he in? And do he got a bond?" "I don't know if he got bond, but he's locked up in Alabama."

I thought, *how in the hell did he get to Alabama when the trip was from Tennessee to Georgia*?! That didn't make any damn sense but I was definitely going to pay him a visit. Since we were advancing in the tournament, going to see him was going to be even harder. I didn't want to talk too much to Corey on the phone. I didn't know if he was in there telling or what. So it had to be a face to face meeting. Corey was a pretty solid dude, but you can't predict how a person acts under certain circumstances. Pressure busts pipes, and with over 1,000 pills and all that compressed weed, Corey was definitely facing a trafficking charge.

When I finally got to see Corey in jail, it broke my heart! I felt like it was my fault. Shit it was my fault. It was déjà vu all over again: my package, his car. This was all too familiar. It was nearly the same scenario as when I got locked up. A little different because I didn't know about my brother having drugs in the car, but the same, more or less. There I was involving my best friend in my own personal shit. Then I thought about the fact that he had a baby on the way.

The look Corey wore on his face through that glass window on our visit will haunt me forever! His face was all sunken in from not eating that nasty county food. He had bags under his eyes from not sleeping, looked like he had the flu, and his face was all scruffy like he hadn't shaven in months.

I couldn't take a painful ass visit so I decided to lighten up the tension and make him laugh.

"Damn my nigga. It only been a week and some change! They ain't gonna believe you innocent if you look like a criminal!"

Corey smirked and replied, "Fuck you! I got to get up outta here! I'm aight though. I just feel like a gold fish in this orange suit, trying not to bump into nobody!"

We chopped it up for as long as we were allowed. I let him know that I already put down a retainer fee for his lawyer. My whole purpose for the visit was to check on my homeboy. But I also wanted to feel him out and see how his vibe was. I basically had to check him out because outside of Brandon, he was the one person who could bring my fairytale with basketball to an end!

Sitting around people trying to control all the emotions, thoughts, and feelings became overwhelming. I was usually mellow and relaxed in all situations but that soon changed to stressed and depressed. I went from smiling and joking around to throw people off, to searching for a reason to smile. I felt like a slave to the days! From sun up to sun down, my thoughts got the best of me.

I looked like a zombie in practice. I sat out most days leading up to the Elite 8, with threats of dehydration and migraines. The Elite 8 didn't seem nearly as much of a big deal as the Sweet 16. I mean we already beat the favorites to win the whole tournament. Up next we had to play Kansas.

Two days before the game, Corey had his first preliminary hearing. That was going to determine if he had a bond and would let us know what type of time he was facing. The state of Kentucky had more than enough evidence to force a trial and Corey knew that. He was caught red handed. Kentucky was a commonwealth state, too. That means they made up their own laws. Since Corey already had a criminal history, the state of Kentucky was going to come down on him! They were a lot stricter just to set an example.

The courts ended up offering Corey a plea deal. He decided not to take it to trial because with the risk of being found guilty, he stood a minimum of 10 years in prison. With the plea deal, he would get half that time and be eligible for parole after three years. To make matters even worse, Corey's baby ended up dying in the hospital. The pain was unbearable. I felt like I was the cause of all of it. Granted, I didn't have anything to do with his child passing away. Shit, I didn't even have anything to do with him going off to Kentucky to try to pick up another package. But I was the one who introduced him to the hustling shit lifestyle and I felt like this was the sum result of all my bullshit. The pain was eating away at me. I became paranoid because I saw firsthand how only a couple of weeks in jail affected Corey and I thought he was going to break. By break I mean tell on me to get him less time. Corey gave these weird facial expressions and made little side comments that led me to believe that if he had the opportunity to tell, he would. I knew it would've been my word versus his, but given all the things he actually knew about how I operated, the judge would've believed him. That would've been enough to open up an investigation at least.

I thought about the shit so much that I had literally convinced myself that it was only a matter of time. I let Brandon know how I was feeling and that's when he told me all the shit Corey's girlfriend was saying. Come to find out, Corey was one hell of a pillow talker. He told his chick things he should've just kept to himself. I mean damn near in full detail. Where he fucked up at though was leading her to believe that he was the mastermind behind the whole operation. You know how people can be, trying to make them look better or be more important than what they really are. This confirmed my suspicion! I made $20,000 off the last game when I put down $2,000 for the 10-to-1 odds. So even though I lost my package, I had enough money to give El Capo that month and enough to re-up with another package.

Everything in me was telling me to not re-up because things were hot, but when I thought about my brother, that was more than enough reason. Corey was so close to me that he knew my pick up dates. He didn't know the location because I always went back home myself. I made sure I made face to face meetings with Knowledge just in case something like this happened. Of course I didn't tell Knowledge what was going on because I didn't want to scare him off or make him feel like I didn't have control of my situation. Instead, I told him I was going to change my pick up dates to after the Elite 8 Kansas game. That way I would have the perfect alibi and I could see if Corey was in jail snitching or anything.

Brandon chilled at our usual pick up spot. Only this time, there were no packages being dropped off or anything illegal going on. It was literally just Brandon being my ears and eyes.

As we arrived to the game, being escorted by the cops and security had me paranoid! I was daydreaming about the police locking my ass up in the middle of the game. After all the success we had up until this point, I guess the people making the odds for the game took us serious. They had to be because the odds were damn near even entering the game. That made it pointless for me to make an anonymous bet.

Going into the game, I felt like shit and was damn near lifeless. My mind just wasn't into the game and it showed. My body language was so bad that my coach benched me. That had to be the worst game of my life. Truth be told, I really didn't give a fuck. I had other shit to worry about. We lost that game to Kansas by 15 points and our run was over. I had 4 points and 4 turnovers! In the post-game press conference, I didn't say much. Seeing my teammates ball up and literally cry at every question asked was just heartbreaking and irritating to me. It was heartbreaking because I know all the hard work and preparation we put into making it as far as we did. All those early morning sprints and three hour practices were out of the window.

I let my troops down.

We knew damn well we played better then Kansas. I just didn't have it that night. And since I was the leader, I took full responsibility.

Without being asked a question I just took the mic.

"Excuse me! Excuse me! Excuse me! I know I don't really say much, and when I do it's something random and outspoken. I just want to speak on a serious note right now though. I say this specifically to my teammates, coaching staff, and every fan and supporter or our program." I turned to my teammates. "I'm sorry! I let y'all down! Today, I just didn't have it!! I watched y'all fight from the bench and that hurt just as much as seeing y'all cry right now. I felt helpless, and that's a pain nobody should experience."

What started as a simple apology to my teammates turned into a full out emotional spill with tears coming down my eyes. My teammates deserved to know why the hell my mind wasn't in the game, but I knew it would jeopardize everything. Keeping that bottled up inside brought on death-like migraines. My nose even started to bleed. That's why it was so irritating. Usually, I would handle pain by getting away from everybody.

But right then and there, I felt like they were forcing me to feel these feelings.

We went home the next day and it was back to reality. Brandon told me nothing suspicious had happened. That meant Corey wasn't saying shit in jail. Or at least not yet. Even though things seemed in the clear, somebody could've been watching the whole time and Brandon just didn't know. So I decided to switch it up and push back my package even further.

I was paranoid, but I wasn't stupid.

A couple weeks went by and the tournament was long over. Despite my last game, I made a big enough impact to be predicted as a lottery pick in the NBA draft. My coach sat me down and met with me. He basically encouraged me to enter the draft because my stock was so high.

"King, I've been hard on you since the day you got here. For a number of reasons but mostly to push you. When I look at you, I see a young man that has been blessed with many physical gifts and talents, but these stretch far beyond basketball. I watched you how you lead this team and took on every challenge this year. You took us all on your back and became an inspiration. You sustained a 3.5 or higher GPA through all the adversity you faced. I look at you and just can't figure you out. You are unique! You are special! Don't waste your talents! Don't waste your talents!"

As he said 'don't waste your talents', he looked at me right in my eyes. He said it as if he knew or had some idea of what I had going on in the streets. Maybe this was my paranoia, but Coach definitely meant something by what he said.

I left coach's office knowing it was time to enter the NBA draft, and trying to figure out how to make all this side shit stop. I kept putting off my trip to go re-up because I didn't know if it was a set up. I mean, there was no way Corey even knew about Knowledge and our thing, but when someone gets locked up in that type of situation, you question everything! Sitting back viewing all the pros and cons I thought to myself, *Corey got caught in Alabama but I was going to Georgia.* He didn't know the other side about how my operation was working so there wasn't too much he could tell.

I went on about my day as usual. Debating back-and-forth on whether I should leave or not. I finally convinced myself and set it up for me to take that trip the upcoming weekend. The season was over so I didn't have to plan around my basketball schedule which was way better. The night before my trip, I said a long prayer. I prayed so long, that I ended up falling asleep while I was still praying without realizing. As I prayed, tears rolled down my eyes. I had both hands together, eyes shut tight, and my knees on the floor. It was more so like I was having a conversation with God. It wasn't your typical conversation or prayer though because I didn't ask for blessings or forgiveness. Instead, I gave my reasons for doing the things I did. I was telling God how I saw things through my eyes. I was angry, scared, confused, stressed the fuck out mentally and just lost!

All these emotions came out passionately while I was praying.

"Father, this free will ain't that free huh? Especially when every decision comes with a price! Right or wrong, you knew my path before I chose it. So it's only fair to judge my heart over my actions. I'm lost and tangled in a way that I created and I can admit that. I don't understand all the 'whys' as far as things happening in my life, nor do I question them. I just find my logic in doing the wrong things for the right reasons. I know you're there. I can feel your presence in every smile I crack knowing all the things I made it through. I don't want to live like this! This ain't me! It's as simple as you showed me a problem and I tried to create an answer. I was born out of love, but quickly exposed to pain. Eventually you learn how to cope. Surprising feelings became key to my survival. Now I just feel numb."

I prayed for at least an hour and a half. Before I knew it, I was asleep. I woke up, took a shower, ate some breakfast, and hit the road.

VII

Traveling early was the best way so I could beat traffic. About 45 minutes into the drive, I stopped to get some gas. That's when I realized I forgot my wallet. Damn! I thought to myself. I can't drive back to get it. That's damn near an hour away. And then I thought I would run into morning traffic but I decided to go back anyway. Because I knew it would be just my luck! So I drove back to school just to get my wallet. I ran into traffic like I thought. I started to think that shit was a sign but I pushed through anyway. The ride was smooth getting there besides the traffic there wasn't a lot of highway patrol out.

Since I arrived later than scheduled, I ended up having to wait for Knowledge.

Knowledge was a smooth nigga usually, but something was a little off about him when we finally met up. He seemed jittery, but I tried to think nothing of it. We had our usual exchange. I brought him a book bag full of money and we would chop it up and talk shit in his condo. While he counted the money on his money machine, my truck would be getting loaded simultaneously.

Knowledge didn't trust anyone but his girl. She held him down while we were locked up so I knew she was official. She was the one in the private parking garage loading my car up. That gave me an idea.

I met up with Lorraine earlier that day while waiting for Knowledge. She had gotten a new job so she was there for the weekend looking for a house. I tried to convince her to drive back with me but she convinced me to spend the weekend with her. Even exchange. The weekend came to an end. Before we left, we stopped to get some breakfast at Waffle House. Lorraine wasn't too talkative, so of course I asked what was wrong.

"I want to know the real reason you want me to follow you to the school, King. I mean, you didn't even know I was here," she said to me.

"We didn't plan it, but I'm glad that you are! I stayed the weekend because I wanted to spend some time with you. The season is over as you know so I got a little time on my hands. I'm going to enter the draft, Lorraine. That's an exclusive for you right there," I replied.

"Oh yeah! Well done! You killed the tournament. Congratulations!" Lorraine excitedly said.

"Thank you kindly! I appreciate that but listen – I came down here on my money shit." "Money shit!? What you mean money shit?"

"Look, I don't want to lie to you! And I don't feel comfortable telling you too much more. My older brother got into it with the wrong people in prison and I'm just trying to help him. That's the God's honest truth; I'm not out here robbing people, killing people, none of that crazy shit. I'm just trying to deliver a package. I trust you! If something happens to me and I can't deliver the package, you can let the right people know what's going on!"

"Who the hell is the right people?"

"I'll tell you when you need to know. Now ain't the time. You might not even need to know. Since you are passing through Tennessee to get to Kentucky, I figured why not have you follow me."

Lorraine gave me a little side eye and attitude, but she followed me anyway. We were in separate cars. So about an hour into the trip, we stopped to get some gas. As we pulled up to the gas station, Lorraine got a flat tire. I thought to myself, shit, I do not need this right now! Lucky enough, she had a good spare and jack in her car so I was able to change it myself.

Lorraine had no idea what exactly the package was; She thought I was transporting money. That's all she needed to know. We stopped at a hotel close to the gas station because she refused to use the gas station's bathroom. Lorraine said that the Waffle House flu was running through her, so I knew she was going to take a while. I waited in the car for about 30 minutes and then we left.

When we got back on the highway, there was a little traffic. That was good for me because I liked merging with traffic; It made it easier to blend in because seeing out of town plates was a red flag for highway patrols.

As we got closer to campus, we ran into a roadblock. They were doing construction on the highway so we were forced into a detour. That detour led us straight into a police roadblock. The officer told me they were looking for drunk drivers since it was Cinco de Mayo. We were in a college town, so I understood. I played it cool and fully cooperated with the officer, even though I was nervous as hell. My license was clean and I was in a fully insured rental car. I wasn't speeding and my seatbelt was on. I had nothing to worry about. There was no need for this officer to check my car and find anything. My license was checked out and I wasn't drinking so the officer let me pass through. I was relieved, but I also saw a couple of unmarked cars on the side of the road. I waited till Lorraine got through as well.

A couple miles up the highway I noticed a car approaching pretty damn fast in my rearview mirror. I didn't think anything of it, but the closer it got, the more I realized it was one of those unmarked cars.

My heart started pounding out of my chest!

I didn't want to overreact because they very well could not be paying me any attention. But the closer the car got, the slower time seemed to pass by. It was a four lane highway so I moved two lanes over to the right. I wanted to first get out of the way, and secondly see what they were going to do. The unmarked, all black SUV got over two lanes as well. I sped up a little bit to see if they would speed up to keep pace with me. They sped up as well. Then I passed an unmarked Dodge Charger. It shot onto the highway quick and was right behind the black SUV! The Charger got in front of the SUV and got closer to my car.

I saw all this shit in the rearview mirror that's when I thought to myself, I'm going to get over two lanes to the left. And if this Charger gets over, I'm out!

I got over and soon as I did, so did the Charger. I floored it! A quarter-mile separated my freedom for the next 10 years. So I hit the gas and got on about my business. I didn't plan on taking them on a high-speed chase; I just wanted to take any attention away from Lorraine.

I was texting Lorraine when I noticed a black SUV following me. I gave her Brandon's number and address and told her that he would know exactly what to do. I hit "send" when the charger got on my ass. I knew Corey's ass was snitching! He had to have said something for these people to know something and start following me out of nowhere.

Good thing I thought quickly on my feet. After about three exits of fleeing the police, I decided to slow down. Lorraine was off the highway and headed where she needed to be.

I was just creating a diversion.

When we stopped at the gas station about an hour back, I put the package in her car where her spare tire went. To her, it looked like I was just changing her tire so it worked out fine and she was completely clueless. But to me, I started thanking God for that flat tire! Brandon already knew what to do once Lorraine got there. Lorraine still thought it was only money I had with me. She had no way of knowing that I put the package of pills and weed in her car. When Brandon pulled the duffel bag out of her car, she still thought it was money. I let Brandon know, the less she knew, the better. I had finally pulled over because I didn't have a reason to keep running. I was clean and Lorraine was safe. I figured Corey was going to fold under the pressure and interrogations in jail, so I prepared for this scenario weeks ago. I knew it was just a matter of time.

As I was pulling over from the police, I hit a pothole along the emergency exit. I was going about 75 mph so my tire busted and I lost control of the car. The car flipped back into oncoming traffic. Usually when you don't have a seatbelt on in an accident this tragic, it often results in life lost. In my case, not having a seatbelt on saved my life. I was thrown out of the car as it flipped four times. A bruised tailbone and some random cuts and wounds were the extent of my injuries until a small explosion shot glass in my eyes.

My eyes were on fire.

It felt like someone had stabbed me in both of my eyes. The plastic from the contacts I had on melted on my eyes and the glass and debris cut my sclera, the white part of your eyeball. I was in so much pain.

After three days of surgery, the doctors repaired my eyes as much as they could but I still ended up with pretty much the worst outcome: I was legally blind. I could see nothing but darkness. When I touched my eyes, they were covered in bandages. The psychological pain of not being able to see drove me crazy! It would've been different or easier to cope with if I had been born blind and never saw anything. Instead, I had all these images and memories in my head of things I had experienced.

I cried daily. Lorraine's voice and the resonance of my family was the only thing that calmed me down. Being blind felt like being in space all by my damn self. Everything was dark!

My only guidance outside of Lorraine and my family was from the voices I heard from the nurses. I decided to focus on colors. I would have any and everyone who came to visit me, including my nurses, describe in full detail what was going on around me. I would ask what people had on, what the weather looked like outside, even the colors from the TV shows. My head was constantly hurting!

The stress and pressure of trying to deal with things were getting to me. I was having anxiety attacks all the time. Sometimes the doctor would strap me to the hospital bed because I would actually get up and move around in my dreams.

Three months passed and I started getting used to the struggle. I had a heightened sense of all things outside of my vision. It was like every other sense pitched in extra because of my lack of vision.

I could recognize and smell what was for breakfast, lunch, and dinner because there was a vent over my bed. I knew what nurse or visitors I had from the sounds of their shoes clicking on the floor. I even knew when

Lorraine spent the night because she would hold my hand and I could feel her pulse. She had an awkward heartbeat.

One day Lorraine came to visit me with Brandon. I knew something was wrong because when I held her hand, her normal awkward heartbeat was different. I asked several times what was wrong but they were both quiet. I could feel Lorraine crying.

Her tears rolled down her face and onto mine.

Then she whispered to me, "They found your brother dead in his cell last night, King! He was stabbed and died from a punctured lung."

I was speechless. I went numb. Shocked wasn't the word. I fell into an immediate feeling of guilt and just started yelling. That yelling turned into me getting up and throwing whatever I could get my hands on. Cursing, screaming, and crying were just some of my reflexive actions.

I dropped the ball.

My brother was actually dead because of me. El Capo didn't receive a couple of payments and took matters into his own hands. Brandon was trying to make moves for me the best he could, but without me giving him my plug, there was only so much he could do. Brandon was just as scared as I was. We knew it was Corey snitching and it was only a matter of time before they came looking for him. That made it hard to make any moves, so I knew he was just selling weed here and there. After a long conversation, I finally convinced Brandon to get the hell away from that country college town.

Visiting time was over. The doctors cleaned up the mess I made and injected me with my daily shot to help me relax and fall asleep, even though that was nearly impossible with all the shit that was on my mind. A couple hours went by and I felt my body literally sinking into the bed. I called for the nurses and told them how I was uneasy and unable to rest. I made up a bunch of shit so they would stay in the room with me. I was scared!

If El Capo was behind my brother being stabbed in prison, then I knew I was next! I kept wondering how the hell could I defend myself from something I couldn't see coming!? El Capo was so connected. He probably had a guard stab my brother.

Things were fine for about an hour.

The nurses calmed me down and assumed I had fallen asleep. When they left, a new set of nurses came to work. I could hear them clearly in the hallway. They assigned some new guy to my room who was just filling in for some other nurse who was sick that night. When the last shift of nurses gave me dinner, I kept my metal fork under my pillow. I wanted to take the knife but they would have noticed that was missing. As the new male nurse approached me, I slid my hand under my pillow. I counted the steps towards me.

My heart raced more and more as he got closer.

Right when he was above me. I dropped my fucking fork! As soon as the fork hit the ground, I jumped up off the hospital bed and ran towards the door! I ran out causing a huge scene and had to be restrained by over 10 people.

I was scared shitless! If it was meant for somebody to kill me that night, I was going to make it hard for them! The security guards and nurses held me down and strapped me to the hospital bed. While I was laying there, they gave me another shot. This massive needle full of anxiety medicine nearly put me straight to sleep. I was already drowsy and fighting my sleep, but that shot almost worked immediately. I needed it.

Everything was already dark, but I could see this bright white light floating around. I'm not sure where it was from, but it was above my head. It was the only thing I had seen in months so I concentrated on the light. It floated around and then dropped on my shoulder.

As soon as the light touched me, I went into a deep sleep. It felt like my body was being teleported. Like I was moving at the speed of light. I only knew I was moving at the speed of light because the light told me. I was clueless as to where this light was taking me, but as I looked around, I noticed that I could see colors.

I was traveling through space, or at least that's what it looked like. They were the brightest stars I had ever seen! The colors were beautiful. The pinks and purples made up skies as I traveled through the universe. I was literally in space. I could see it. Planets and galaxies full of life that I could feel. I was more like an energy than a being.

Being blind made me consciously aware that I was dreaming because of the things I could see. The medical term for this is lucid dreaming. In other words, I was awake in my sleep. Things got gloomy and only flashes of white and black took over. I could feel myself being pulled through a tunnel like shape. It felt like riding on a roller coaster at an indescribable speed while looking through a kaleidoscope at the same time. The only thing that could move this fast is energy.

Things really got weird when I noticed myself looking at my own energy. It's hard to explain, but I went into another world, another dimension, another reality, but ended up in that same hospital room. As I looked at myself on the hospital bed, I realized that the light that dropped on my shoulder before was there again.

When it hit my body, I woke up. I was still dreaming because I could see everything clearly. It was a bright ass day and I noticed it was snowing. The curtains were wide open and a blanket of snow covered the city. Awkward movements in the clouds caused me to stare into the sky. They were moving in unique patterns that I couldn't quite make out. The clouds looked fake, but so real at the same time. It was almost as if you could touch them. I thought to myself, damn, that's some good ass shit in that shot they gave me! Got me thinking I'm teleporting and shit! Then I noticed that these clouds were moving at an indescribable speed.

But then suddenly, I was mesmerized by how the whole sky cleared. There were no more clouds in sight. I did a complete 360 degree scan of the sky and couldn't find a single cloud! It appeared that way for at least five minutes.

Then, out of nowhere appeared this lifelike UFO mothership big enough for the whole world to see. It was in the form of a cloud like image.

I knew there was only one thing I could be seeing. I saw God! I knew it was God because of the feelings that raced through my body almost immediately upon site.

I went from feeling startled and scared to invited and loved! The image moving as the cloud above seemed to be looking directly at me. The eyes were piercing. There was a deep dark fog with a piercing blue diamond like dot for the eyes. The face was so detailed that you knew it was more than a cloud image. You could see the nose, eyes, ears and crown that he wore on his head. The beard and facial features were just as detailed. I knew exactly what I was looking at.

I dropped to my knees and started praying. As I prayed, tears of joy and feelings of relief overwhelmed me. He spoke to me telepathically. Everything I wanted to know or needed to know was answered immediately. Before I could even question why things happened to me, I already had my answers. It was weird. Kind of like I was omniscient.

I didn't want to wake up! It was if I had access to everything. I stayed in that position until the image went away. I figured it was the end of the world but when I looked into the sky, it was leaving.

A snowflake was all that remained as it came down slowly from the sky.

But this wasn't your ordinary snowflake. It was lit up, changing colors from white to sky blue. Sort of like a flickering light. The window was closed but the snowflake dropped in right through the walls. It made a very slow, dramatic, drawn out entrance, but once the snowflake hit the ground, it changed immediately to a dog. I couldn't make out what kind of dog it was, but when he jumped on me, I woke up from my dream.

Lorraine was in my room, I could hear her heartbeat. I couldn't see any more so I knew it was back to my reality. My dream felt so real. I wanted to tell Lorraine about it but I was so discouraged to know I was blind again. All the answers, access to information, feelings and emotions I had in my dream were real. They were so detailed that I couldn't believe that that was just a dream. I was confused and lost. I felt like God spoke to me directly in my dream like I had always prayed would happen. The clarity from answers he gave me were so strong.

I decided to keep my dream to myself.

Lorraine stayed for a couple more hours but I could tell she was itching to leave. The whole time she was there, I didn't say much. My thoughts were consumed by my dream.

Lorraine recognized my mind was elsewhere, which was probably why she decided to leave early.

Before she left, she told me she had a surprise for me.

"I know it gets lonely in here, King, I just wanted to bring you a friend to keep you company. What's better than a man's best friend?"

That's when I heard scratching and whimpering. It could've been anything. Lorraine was very silly and always had practical jokes so I didn't know what to expect. When she opened the box a puppy jumped right on me and started licking my face.

It was a Seeing Eye Dog. It wasn't a regular Seeing Eye Dog though. As I rubbed the dog and asked Lorraine to describe it to me, I realized it was the same dog from my dream! It was the snowflake. There was no possible way Lorraine knew about my dream so that gave me confirmation.

What I had dreamed about really happened.

All of those feelings and emotions, colors and scenery were actually true.

That made me believe I was going to see again. Which also meant I had to change my state of mind. You see, when I was dreaming, I got an answer to every question I had ever asked. Even the difficult questions that I didn't necessarily want an answer to. Without me even thinking, those answers were placed in my mind. It was like a timeline. From me going to jail to me going blind, I had all the answers as to why things happened to me. I even knew why my mother passed away and I could actually feel her energy. It wasn't just a dream! And if it were, my belief in it was so strong that I was willing to be convinced otherwise.

I learned through my dream that I had actually chosen this life.

We never die, none of us. We are all made of energy and that can't be destroyed. It's quantum physics. I could understand it clear as day through my dream. Our thoughts are also energy. I was able to see my thoughts in wave patterns. Sort of like a radio frequency. The waves transformed from waves to particles and joined together at harmonious frequencies. This shaped my whole life's experience in the physical world. Energy is the only thing faster than the speed of light. That's because it doesn't travel, it is interconnected with all other energy.

The universe is nothing but a huge vibrating ball of interconnected energy with the ability to communicate into infinity with no regard to space and time. So basically, I chose this life. I chose this pain. My free will made up my reality. Just like I chose to change that pain into basketball all of those years. My reality was shaped through my thoughts.

Those thoughts and visions weighed so heavily on me that I wanted to talk to somebody about all of the knowledge that had been placed in my brain. I knew nobody would believe me or even take what I was saying serious, so I decided to keep it to myself. Instead, I was going to put the info to use. I concentrated daily on exactly how I wanted my life to be. I could even visualize the waves going off into the universe. The deep, specific thoughts turned into me going into meditations! The hospital kept me doing tests so I had nothing but time on my hands. I didn't watch TV and if I didn't have a visitor, I would listen to audiobooks about meditating. Instead of music, I would listen to peaceful sounds of the ocean or nature as I created in my head.

Every morning I woke up, Snowflake and I would walk over to the window. Even though I couldn't see, I would play out in my head exactly what I saw in my dream. Some mornings I fell and stumbled into some things but eventually became routine.

Everything was numbers to me. I knew exactly how many steps it was from my bed to the window. I could tell the time by the four different nurse shifts or my 4 p.m. visitors because visiting hours were from 4 to 7 p.m. The nurses would catch me with my window open and standing in front of it every day! When they asked what I was doing, I would tell them I was looking at the clouds. Of course they had jokes and thought I was crazy, but all that changed after about a year.

It was a typical morning, I woke up and did my regular thing. As I stood in front of the window and gave thanks, a new nurse walked in my room.

"Good morning, King! I'm Nurse Hope. I'm filling in for Nurse Johnson and taking her morning shift."

"Hope? Is that your real name or some cool doctor nickname?" "Well, that's actually my real name. Is King yours?"

"Yeah, and Hope is a really cool name."

"What are you doing by the window?" She asked me.

"The sun is so bright right now. Looks like it's going to be a good ass day. But I can see that it's going to rain a little later. I can smell it. Plus my knee is sore so I know it's coming!"

Nurse Hope paused for a minute. Then I heard some movement in the room. She picked up my chart.

"According to this chart, you're sightless, King! How can you see the sun and know that it's going to rain later? Because as you were talking, I was looking out at the sky and could see some dark clouds coming. This is kind of freaking me out. How can you do that?!"

Before I could answer her question, I started getting dizzy. I felt a little lightheaded so she helped me to the bed. I didn't have an answer for her. I could just feel it. Lorraine came to visit me that day like she always did, three times a week.

She complimented me on how upbeat and positive I had been lately. That's when I decided to tell her about my dream. It took me the whole visiting time to try to explain things I saw and felt in my dream. I wasn't expecting her to understand, I just wanted to get it out. I even went as far as to tell her about the world I created. Lorraine didn't say much. I know it spooked her out even more when I told her about Snowflake. As she got up to leave, I told her to tie her shoes. She stopped dead in her tracks. She was really freaked out. But that's when she started to believe me.

Over the next couple of weeks, Lorraine would spend all of her visiting time recording me speak. She not only wanted to know more about my dream, but she also wanted me to speak about quantum physics and mechanics and how it relates to life. When Lorraine would leave me, she would write down and put in a book what I was telling her. She used the recordings as the audio side of our book. When the book was finally finished, she would read it back to me and asked for my feedback. Everything was perfect. The only thing she couldn't decide on was the title. Lorraine wanted me to give the book a title before she released it. I told her to let me think about it and that's when she left.

Visiting time was over. She left the audio and the book with me so I could listen to it.

Little did I know, that would be the last time I would ever hear from Lorraine again. That night, Lorraine passed away in her sleep. She was perfectly healthy. When the doctors explained to me what happened, they said she had some form of sleep apnea. Basically she stopped breathing in her sleep. I couldn't wrap my mind around it. She was so happy. She was also part of the world I created so I didn't understand how or why!

I cried myself into a deep sleep, only to find Lorraine sitting there waiting for me. I was totally fucking confused. I knew we never died, but to see her so soon in my dream was so real. We held hands and walked around in my dream which was the actual setting of the world I created! We talked for hours in my dream but actually never said a word. It was all telepathic. I could feel every thought she had.

When I asked Lorraine about her death, she told me she never died. As she said this, the scenery changed. We went from walking to literally dropping into a black hole. The dropping turned into floating. Then strings of color made their way all around me. It formed and banded into cube shapes. It was like I was in an infinite square. It looked like strings of a guitar but stronger like cables from a bridge. The colors were infinite and the cube went in every direction and dimension. It was sort of like I was in a tesseract. A big ass maze with a projection on the other side of each angle. When I focused on the projection, I noticed that they were all me! It was me, passed out on my bed the night before I ever took that last trip out of town. Same outfit, same setting, even the exact same position I was in when

I fell asleep. Whenever I stared long enough at one of the projections, I could see it move and play out different scenarios. It was like it was in tune with my thoughts because once I was locked into a scenario, I could actually feel what was going on in the projection. They were all around me. Infinite possibilities!

I just had to choose the right one. I quickly became overwhelmed as my thoughts cluttered. There were so many different ways to go. The projections only lasted about 10 to 15 seconds but in that time, I felt every emotion as a result of the decision I made. I then realized that I had stepped into some inner source of me. It was all my life! Freewill at its finest. Instead of panicking, I focused on all the things that made me happy. Then I focused on what I wanted my life to be. The cube and projections moved around accordingly. It was like I was literally creating my world. All that extra time to think made it easy to choose which projection to go through. I had already been planning out how I wanted my life. As I looked at this projection, all lit up in colors, I said a prayer. The only thing I asked for was to remember why I chose that projection. When I touched the projection, it became 3D. Not only did it become 3D, but it surrounded me until I saw nothing but a white light.

As the light went away, I felt myself waking up. Only this time, I wasn't in a hospital bed! I was literally back in my room and it was the next day. My alarm went off at 5 a.m. because that's when I was supposed to be hitting the road to make my trip back home to re-up.

I was back!

VIII

Had I been dreaming this whole time?

I ran straight to the front window and looked up at the sky. I was looking for any signs of crazy movements in the clouds. Nothing happened. I ran to the bathroom and looked in the mirror.

I could see! It was really me!

I splashed water on my face and jumped into the shower just thinking I was dreaming. I wanted to wake up but nothing happened. It was weird. Kind of like déjà vu but more intense. I knew my dream happened! Normally, by this time, I would have forgotten what the hell my dream was about. But this time, it lingered on my brain. I even felt different. Like I had a renewed attitude and spirit.

That had to mean the car accident, the police chase causing me to go blind, all of that.

None of it really happened! Most of all, Lorraine's death.

I immediately texted Lorraine, "Good morning, beautiful!"

As I waited for my reply, I got dressed and ate some food. Thirty minutes went by and I still didn't have a reply. When I went outside to my car, one of my neighbors approached me.

"What's up, King! I got Snowflake by the mailboxes while I was jogging. Good thing we got speed bumps because he was in the street and his little ass almost got hit!"

Then he showed me my dog! It was the same dog! My mind was blown. Snowflake jumped in my arms and licked my face the same way he did when I was in the hospital bed. The same dog. I could tell by the eyes.

If this was true and reality, then what I dreamed about had to be true, too. I still needed a little more proof. I thought maybe I could have just been tripping.

My phone rang and it was Brandon.

"Just the nigga I need to talk to! I had the craziest fucking dream. I am on my way to your house now!" I said to him.

Then Brandon cut me off and said, "I was on my way to your house now! I wanted to talk to you about some shit face to face! Meet me somewhere."

The first thing that came to mind was Corey. I figured Brandon was going to update me on his case status or something.

We met up at Waffle House and before I could get a word out, he told me Lorraine had died the night before. She was in a fatal car accident. Lorraine had an epileptic seizure while driving back home traveling for work. She drove off the road.

That was all I needed to hear to get the hell up and leave! Brandon knew about this because his girlfriend and Lorraine were in the same sorority. I didn't need details. I was in disbelief. I found myself staring at my phone on the side of the highway crying. Waiting on Lorraine to text me back. None of that shit made sense!

Was I still fucking dreaming? If everything I felt and knew about my dream was true, then why would I have chosen this reality? A reality without Lorraine? It just didn't add up.

I called Knowledge to let him know I wasn't feeling too good, and that I wasn't going to make that trip. I drove home, hurt and distraught. My mind was puzzled and my emotions were numb. The funeral was later that week and I couldn't sleep at all leading up to that day. I took a couple of cat naps throughout the day, but for the most part, I probably only slept a total of six hours in four whole days. I was hurt of course because Lorraine was gone, but I was consumed more on why I made the decision for that scenario to be my reality. I felt like I was mad at myself.

Right before the funeral started, without giving me any early notice, Lorraine's brother asked me to speak during the funeral. My initial response was a hell no. That took strength that I didn't want to have at the time. I needed the time to mourn. It was my baby's death. I loved that girl with everything I had in me and I even planned on making her my Queen. I didn't understand and I didn't want to understand.

As the funeral proceeded, my emotions calmed. Lorraine's presence was definitely in the room. The climate changed at least three times from heavy rain to a light rain, to complete sun light. As I looked around the church, I thought about all of the lives Lorraine had impacted with her presence. It was a relaxing feeling. That's when Lorraine's mother took the stage, and asked if I would come up to share some words. My initial reaction was another no, but I didn't want to look like an asshole being put on the spot like that.

As I made my way towards the stage, I got nervous. The casket had been closed the whole time up until this point. They opened it as I took the podium. I stared right in her face. I went into a daydream for however long, crying and just looking at Lorraine. She was beautiful. As I tried to speak, nothing would come out. It was like I was stuck. Just blank. Then everyone disappeared. I blocked everyone out and walked towards Lorraine's body. I spoke to her as if it were just her and I in there. I told her that was a pain that I'm glad she didn't have to experience. I didn't want to hold up the funeral so I kept my word brief.

When I went back to my seat, I opened the eulogy for the first time. There were several pictures and memories of Lorraine throughout the program, but one stood out more than others. It was an old Halloween picture of Lorraine from when she was a kid. She had to be about eight years old and she was dressed as an angel in all white. Under her picture read, "Remember why you are here!" Those words jumped off the page to me.

As the funeral concluded and they were lowering Lorraine's casket into the ground, I threw a rose down. It was a white rose. The white rose was a symbol of new life and a new journey. As I watched them lower her, it hit me.

Remember why you're here! Remember why you're fucking here, I thought to myself. It was clear as day! Nothing had ever been clearer. I thought back to the maze-like infinite square from my dream. It was all coming back to me. I remembered everything.

I chose this reality because Lorraine's death was the only way I was going to know that my dream was real. When I prayed before I entered it, I remembered asking to have the ability to retain everything I learned, and to be able to believe it. It was all so true.

Chills rushed through my body!

I promised Lorraine that her death wouldn't go in vain as I left. I remembered the book she was putting together from my dream and immediately started writing it. It was based on all the information I gave her so I finished it the same way she started it. I would tie a thick bandage around my eyes and record myself talking for hours.

Time went by and it was time to pay El Capo a visit. I had enough on my own to pay him out of pocket, so that month's debt was taken care of. We spoke about me and the NBA and he agreed that I could pay him later. I owed him $50,000. El Capo just said the longer he waited, the more he was going to expect on the interest. That was understandable. It would buy me time and his goons wouldn't be down my throat. As ruthless as his cartel was known to be, I'm just glad he agreed to give me some time.

Later on that week, I drove to Alabama to pay Corey a visit. We needed to have a man-to-man, heart to heart talk. I needed him to know my concerns and also my intentions. Visiting time was only about 20 minutes so I didn't waste any time! Corey knew I was scared of him telling on me and turning us in because I told him about what he did in my dream! I also let him know about Lorraine's death and how that's what I woke up to. I even told him about entering the draft early. By the time the visit was over, I was convinced that Corey and I were on the same page.

The coaching staff at my school set up a press conference for the media and all other sports writers to come out. That was supposed to be my official announcement for declaring myself eligible for the NBA Draft. I waited till the last minute to hold the press conference because ever since I woke up from my dream, my book was the only thing that consumed my mind and time.

Night in, night out, all day, and every day was another opportunity for me to write more!

It was much more than me actually writing though. I felt like I was shaping my life. The pain became my voice much like how I thought basketball once was. I loved basketball! It literally changed my life. I channeled all the pain I had in my life into positive energy. That's what made me so good in basketball. When I took the theories of my dream and applied it to my own life, it made perfect sense. I was the creator! The things that took place in my life, negative or positive, were all a result from different energies from the law of attraction. The press conference platform was the perfect time for me to put what I had learned to use.

The press conference was held in our schools gym. It was packed to capacity. There were students, local fans, media, sports writers, news etc. all in attendance because the press conference was open to the public. As I took the microphone, I looked around the room one last time and thought to myself how basketball connected us all. As I began to speak, instead of talking about basketball I decided to talk about my dream!

"I want to thank everybody who came out today to support me."

I never was known in the past for taking the humble approach when it came to the media, so I knew my press conference was going to get extensive coverage. After talking about my dream and Lorraine's death, I shocked the world!

"I will not be entering this year's NBA draft. I will be returning to school next semester, but only as a student and not as a student athlete! I don't love the game as I once did and just like someone told me in the past, I have other gifts to offer the world!!"

Even though I actually did still love basketball, I knew that the press conference platform was big enough to shake some shit up. I caused a complete uproar! Some people were confused about me not going to the NBA, especially because I was predicted to be a top five pick. The Atlanta Hawks had the number three pick and needed a guard so more than likely, that's where I would have gotten drafted. Some students were mad because I wasn't going to play for my school anymore.

When everyone calmed down, I opened the floor for questions.

"King, what do you plan on doing with yourself since you're not playing basketball anymore?"

I paused for a minute. The conversation I had with El Capo played through my head. As I approached the question, a piece of light from outside shone to the back of the room. Nobody was over in that area where the light shone, but I looked outside, I noticed some mammatus clouds outside. They were the same way the clouds formed in my dream when I went to the hospital window.

When I was writing my book and doing research, I learned the name of these clouds. Then, after about 5 to 10 seconds, the skies cleared again like nothing happened.

I just smiled. Then it all started making sense. This was the perfect setting to not only plug my book, but to put the theory to use. If we all are made of energy and connected by this through a higher power, then that meant that subconsciously they all were going to help me. This was the perfect time to speak on my book.

"I plan on writing a book and turning it into a movie! I'll play basketball again when I fall back in love with it!"

I didn't know what the reaction would be after that. It really wasn't my concern. After the press conference, there were mixed emotions about my decision, but I didn't care. Before I left, a group of people approached me. Some were students, some were adults. They all had the same question though: "Where can I buy your book?"

Later that day, I was all over the TV. I was the talk of the sports world again! People were not just talking about my decision not to go to the NBA, but they were also talking about my new career with me becoming an author. There were plenty of jokes, but it all came to an end when I finally released my book!

I self-published the book and promoted it myself as well. Basketball made me pretty popular which made it easy for my book to go viral. My campus sold out of my book in two hours. I partnered with them so I could sell it out of the bookstore. Ironically, after selling out in two hours, I literally profited the same amount I made when I was selling pills and weed around campus! Then I moved on to other campuses around the state. In one month's time, I made over

$50,000. That not only proved my theory true, but it was also enough to pay El Capo for good! I squared things away with El Capo immediately! That problem was taken care of and it was time to live my new life. My book continued to gain momentum as I entered summer school. I stayed true to my word and didn't return that following season as a basketball player. The media coverage that surrounded my decision not to play made my book even more popular. Anytime they spoke of my school that season, they always mentioned me! Not only did they mention me, but they also mentioned my book as well. That free promotion, along with social media, peeked the interest of some really good movie producers.

My email inbox was flooded daily with offers to buy my story to turn it into a movie. After agreeing to a $1 million offer, whoever had jokes and didn't believe in what I was doing definitely couldn't laugh anymore! I graduated early after only three years of college, I was able to graduate with a 3.6 GPA and I made my first million dollars all before my 22nd birthday! My life had completely changed and I changed right along with it. Financially, I was able to start my own business the way I saw it sitting in that hospital bed! I was in love with life, but something was still missing! Aside from Lorraine not being there to physically enjoy this life with me, something else was missing.

It had been almost three years since I picked up a basketball. So I decided to go play with some friends at a local recreation center. No refs, no crowd cheering for me, and no cameras showing my game on TV. Even though we were only playing for the fellowship, my competitive spirit kicked right in. We lost in the best of seven series, four games to three. That loss sat on my brain all week long. I was truly pissed off! I had been a sore loser my whole life, but I wasn't mad about the game. I was more so mad at my performance. Being rusty was an understatement! I was also winded and things didn't feel like they used to.

I decided to call on my old AAU coach. The same one who took custody of me after I was released from jail. We were business partners as I invested money sponsoring his new AAU team. The kids had a game that weekend and I was going to be in town. Coach allowed me to practice with his team during the week leading up to their weekend tournament. It brought back so many memories! I wasn't that much older than the kids so they looked up to me. As the week went on, they got more comfortable with me and began asking questions. Most of which was why I stopped playing basketball. I never lied to the kids. My raw, honest approach was received by them in a way that helped them to look up to me. I took on the big brother/mentor role in their lives. I could feel myself falling back in love with basketball. After about two months of training and conditioning with the kids and on my own, I felt like my normal self. They helped me fall back in love with basketball and I watched them pile on their wings. They had a tournament out in Vegas and of course I went, not only support them, but to also party in Vegas!

There were a lot of familiar faces out there from when I was playing basketball. College coaches were recruiting and sports writers were ranking the players. There were also NBA and other former players from university showing support for their former AAU teams. They all pretty much knew who I was from my college days. When we spoke, they told me to come to the training facility where the pros worked out for an off the record game. It was an open invite so I decided to take them up on their offer. When I walked in the gym, it was literally full of professional basketball players.

It was like an NBA pick-up game. We had real refs and we were playing four quarters. I didn't dominate like some expected me to, but I definitely showed that I could play on that level. The following day, word spread around the gym at the AAU tournament that I was there playing and looking pretty good. Sports writers and even some NBA agents approached me with questions. It felt just like the good old college days. I downplayed it all of course, but I had every intention on showing everybody why I belonged in the NBA in the next game.

From the opening tip, I dominated the game! The NBA players were trying to get in shape and I was already about a month ahead of them as far as training and conditioning went. As the week progressed, I opened a lot of eyes. Not only to the players, but also to some NBA scouts and overseas teams. Before I left Vegas, I had invites to four different NBA training camps, and contract offers from three teams in Russia, Spain, and Greece.

This shit was surreal.

What started as me mentoring young kids at a rec center turned into my long lived basketball dreams. I couldn't believe it. That wasn't nearly as exciting as my kids winning that AAU tournament though. They all played great and had scholarship offers from all types of universities.

Jarvis, a 6'6" combo guard was ranked the highest among this group. Ironically, he had already verbally committed to Alabama Tech. I was more proud of him because Jarvis came from more extreme circumstances out of the group. He opened up to me while I was mentoring him. I decided to take one of the NBA teams up on their offer and went to training camp with them about a month later. When I walked through the doors of the practice facility I got chills. That feeling was indescribable! My heart was racing. It started beating so fast that I got a little lightheaded. Five deep breaths and I was good to go. Walking into the locker room and finally seeing my name on an NBA jersey brought me to tears immediately. They were tears of joy of course, but tears nonetheless. A feeling of relief! A satisfaction that I yearned for my whole life. I did it! Then I took some pictures with my phone to remember that moment. After that, it was back to business. I didn't make it that far just to be one of them niggas who "made it"! I was there to do work.

The first day of training camp consisted of extreme conditioning and a lot of fundamental drill work. As a rookie, I didn't want to step on any toes, but as a competitor, I wanted to be among the top of the bunch. I tried to win every drill, offensively and defensively. I even lead the pack when it came to the conditioning part. Just being there had me on an emotional high and gave me all the energy I needed. It was like I wasn't even getting tired. As soon as practice was over, it was a wrap. I had never been more tired in my whole life. I was catching cramps in places that I didn't even know you could catch cramps in. My toes were cramping, my forearms were cramping. I even caught a cramp in my neck. It was an awkward pain, but worth every minute of it. As the week went by, training camp got easier. I guess my body was used to the torture we had to go through. We were going twice a day so I spent my time in the gym, recuperating!

I received a call from my old AAU coach two days before training camp was over. He sounded distraught and damn near crying. When he finally settled down and got out what was going on. I learned that Jarvis was in big trouble. Jarvis had been locked up for murder. It was his senior year and he definitely was on the right track for college. But much like myself, he was in the wrong place at the wrong time. The shit seemed all too familiar! I thought about his situation all night. It bothered me more and more as I thought about it until it eventually brought me to tears! Unable to sleep, I found myself praying for over an hour asking for answers. As I sat there with my eyes closed and in tears, the sun eventually came up.

It was different though.

As the sun came up, it reflected off the hotel mirror and curtains creating an image that was so clear that I knew exactly what I had to do. My vision was a little blurry from having them closed for so long and crying, but when I opened them, I looked in the mirror and I could see a golden circle around my head! As I focused on the golden circle in the mirror, I could also see my shadow through the curtains behind me. It was like my shadow had wings. I thought nothing of it at first except it just to be a simple reflection, until it had been there for over 20 minutes. As I moved, it moved. The golden circle staying on my head and the wings on my back! The golden circle had a burning shining glare with colors that I couldn't explain. The only way to even begin to explain this was a crown, bursting with energy. My immediate thought was I know I'm not no fucking angel, but the feeling that came over gave me complete clarity.

Later that day, I decided to leave training camp. I called a meeting with the coaches and thanked each and every last one of them. With a tear in my eye and a smile on my face, I pulled out of training camp. I went back to where it all started. Jarvis' situation seemed far more important and I felt it needed my personal touch and attention, just as my AAU coach felt my situation needed his.

It took nearly $100,000 of my own personal money in lawyer fees to prove that Jarvis was literally in the wrong place at the wrong time and had absolutely nothing to do with the shooting. The kid literally walked into a store five minutes before it was robbed. The way the media portrayed him before being found innocent on all charges wound up winning Jarvis a settlement that not only paid back my $100,000 but also was enough to pay for Jarvis' college tuition at almost any school! My sole request was for the judge to write a handwritten letter to the school, athletic department, and head coach at Alabama Tech which literally won Jarvis back his full scholarship.

Jarvis had already committed to Alabama Technical University. It was his own decision.

I never tried to influence him in any way when it came down to his school selection. When I asked Jarvis why he decided to choose that school, he looked at me and said, "Alabama Tech was the only school that didn't force money on me! On all my other college visits, they talked about everything else except school and my actual major. I just wanted to pick a school that had my best interest at hand and a no nonsense type of environment!"

That made me grin so big. The similarities between us were scary at times. Moments like that was confirmation that I was doing the right thing by coming back to help this kid out.

Jarvis was a carbon copy of myself. From his personality to his style of play. I kept him under my wing and mentored him throughout his collegiate career. I attended every home game and even flew his parents to the important games out of town. Jarvis became my little brother. Over the next four years, I watched him grow into a man.

Watching Jarvis graduate a semester early brought genuine tears to my eyes, but seeing him shake the NBA commissioner's hand after being drafted was priceless. It was an indescribable feeling. I knew that Jarvis' success was because of a direct decision I made to help change his life. His mother hugged me tight as we both listened to his appreciation speech.

Before he thanked anyone, he spoke directly to me.

With a face full of tears, he looked me directly in the eyes and said, "Thank you! There's no way I could be here without the sacrifices you made for me. Since you came into my life six years ago, you taught me so much about being a man. From prioritizing school, basketball, family, and life. I appreciate you showing me the way. I'm forever in debt but know you don't want anything from me."

He choked up for a second then sniffled his tears away. "Of all the things you taught me, what I'm most thankful for is the understanding of the fundamental difference between a wise man and a smart man. You taught me that a smart man makes a mistake, learns from his mistake, and never makes that mistake again. A wise man finds a smart man and avoids those situations altogether. You're my brother, my mentor, and an even better friend!"

At that moment, as hard as I tried to fight it, tears rolled down my eyes. The profound things he was saying gave me goose bumps. I could hear the authenticity in his voice. That was one hell of a feeling. In fact, it was the same emotional feeling of pure happiness, joy, and competition that I had years ago when I saw what appeared to be God in the sky. That moment made my life seem meaningful. It was clarity and understanding, like I was looking at a puzzle with an aerial view, inserting the last piece.

After celebrating with his family and friends, I went to sleep excited and eager about what tomorrow would bring. Ready to face all challenges and obstacles life was going to throw my way, but with a different attitude.

I prayed aloud right before I went to sleep that night. "Father...... Thank You!"

And then I knocked out.

When the sunlight touched my eyes the next morning, I jumped up! I was full of energy but still half asleep. I wiped the boogers from my eyes and looked around the room. Things looked different.

When my vision cleared, I couldn't believe it. Was I still asleep?! *Am I dreaming?!* I thought to myself.

I woke up in the same exact spot I was in right before I went to re-up that last in my apartment living room from college.

I knew what was going on, I just couldn't believe it! I mean, I could vividly remember before going into that deep sleep asking God to show me another way. Not only did he show me another way, but he also gave me clear discernment in the purest form of why things were. The universe is infinitely perfect, even in all of its destruction. In fact, for any and every problem, there's already a solution. I was shown every decision possibly thought of, already exists in another reality! The way you shake your world is absolutely up to you. After being shown how one small decision can change the course of my life, small decisions weren't so small to me anymore. I knew then, the choice was mine. I put on my clothes, grabbed my keys, and looked to the sky...

KENT GEORGE

ABOUT THE AUTHOR

What's happening world! My name is Kent George. Some may know me as Ravone, some may know me as Ray. Some might even know me from my previous profession which was basketball.

Life is all about progression. I mean, change is inevitable. Change can also be scary than a mafucka. Taking a journey into the unknown causes a sense of discomfort. Me, I'm not daunted by that feeling at all. I understand that nothing worth having comes easy, and I don't fright being great. As I transition from one profession to the next, I invite you all to journey with me as I reinvent myself as an author and a filmmaker.

"King Kent Productions" is my production company that I recently started with a novel I wrote myself titled Divine Intervention being my first project.

Made in the USA
Lexington, KY
28 November 2015